HEADHUNTER101

THROB

Tales of the Heart

First published by Headhunter101 Private Bag 14, Masunga-Botswana email: itsheadhunter101@gmail.com contacts(267 76755513/77516611) 2025

First edition

ISBN: 978-99968-72-07-5

Cover art by SAM D
Advisor: Oratile Aisha Kalake

This book was professionally typeset on Reedsy.
Find out more at reedsy.com

Contents

1

A.C

This is for the woman who gave birth to a fighter, cheers.

2

ACKNOWLEDGMENT

To the Almighty; With each dawn, you infuse me with sheer energy—an electric current that amazes, drives me to the brink of madness, and fills me with boundless joy. Like a celestial compass, your presence guides my steps through life's labyrinth.

And to the one who resides forever in the chambers of my heart: You are more than a friend; you're a force—a gravitational pull toward the summit of my aspirations. Thank you, dear Koala, for being my unwavering companion.

Last, but not least, to those who will champion my journey, who will lift this book upon their shoulders and carry it toward the sun: You are my god, my constellations. Your support fuels my pen, and your belief in my words is the very air I breathe.

With love and absolute madness,

HEADHUNTER101.

3

BOOK QUOTE

"When we were young, the world wasn't such a scary place."
Mad Dog, The Bad Guys.

4

THROB REVIEWS

"I have read it, and I also think your writing style is very
captivating. It gets someone hooked easily
I love how every chapter has its own story to tell
From the chapter on unrequited love to chasing life dreams and
unfulfilled goals ✧
I love it, it's so real"
Oratile Aisha Kalake

This is a compilation of emotions. I was reading different
stories taking the same path that led me to one destination of
understanding. And I am left to ponder one question, What are
we? I'd recommend this book to idealists and millenials.
Generation Beta is blessed because they will be born to meet a
Headhunter masterpiece. Thank you a million times.
Tay-Jay Cannocy(the author of Victim-Birthing Grave.)

"*The humor in this chapter(Monnamogolo) kept me on my toes the whole time the character's frustration a s eventual pride in his unique name is soo entertaining for real, it actually made me root for him...the shift where he wanted to change his name to embracing it is well paced honestly.....*" *Lordshare Ntuka, the author of Silent Sins-Double Betrayal.*

5

FADING CONSTELLATIONS

"For the light, the life, the world you gave me, the love I will carry around like a lantern in the night, Rest In Ultimate Power, Alberto." Headhunter101.

When the star shot through the sky, I'd closed my teary eyes and wished God would grant me blessings and prosperity. I'd wished God had given you an extra decade. Maybe a century or a thousand years like a gumiho. Perhaps an endless life.

But as the ambulance sped in reverse thanks to my disorienta-tion, I'd closed my eyes and counted to thirty before I realized the star that just shot through the sky was you.That was the moment reality really humbled me. You were no longer with me. You will no longer be with me, but you will be the brightest star in the constellation. The star that will shine for eternity. For me. For your twin sister. For everyone else.

You gave me life and snatched it from the tips of my fingers. Away you went with it. Away you flew with it. Flew to a far, far place out of reach. I wouldn't lie, saying I didn't cry. But I'd lied to my friend. She'd asked about the pillow. I told her it was wet because of the hole in my ceiling. I said rain leaked from there.

I'd also told her I was fine. I was not even close to f..i... and I am not fine yet. I am afraid I will never be fine. From time to time, I try to forget, erase you, who God decided to erase from our lives, but I am just there trying the impossible. I swear it will not be easy. You have watched Mission impossible, right? It is that sort.

I have a portrait of you smiling down on me—and weirdly, from all the angles, you are watching me closely, and from all the angles, your smile is still the brightest, warmest I've ever come across in my life. It is like seeing heaven for the first time. For the second time. For the fifth time, and yet you cannot get over the serene and tranquil vibe it gives off.

Somewhere in the middle of my disorientation, I'd asked the driver why we were going back to that place again.

Where you took your last breath.

He'd asked, "Are you sure you are okay?" and I'd just looked at him because at that moment, I couldn't decipher the usual language that seemed like it might have come from Andromeda. I wanted to tell him I was losing my mind. In fact, it was gone for a second? A minute? I'd sobbed quietly and decently, like the person you were.

I'd swear I saw a fire burn. I saw ashes, something disappearing in my eyes until it was no more. The fire was also no more, and when I figured out what could have been burning, I realized it was the moments and memories we shared. They'd turned to ashes and flown by the wind to the far, far place you went. Like the butterflies across the finest fields on Earth. They fly and fly and keep on flapping their wings to farther.

Suddenly, it'd drizzled, and that was after zero o' clock. It rained the following day as well. The following day, too, until after we'd sent you to a better place. That was a sign. That was the goodbye. The "till we meet again" but, now, in a much greater place like heaven.

I'd regretted the "look, I am in a hurry, let's talk on the phone" when you'd suddenly mentioned you wouldn't be here next year, and when we got to the phone, we were like "let's find time and talk in person." That is where we ended, and I hope we will take it from there when we reunite again. Like we always effortlessly found our way to each other without us knowing.

People in buses talked. In shops. At the bus rank. At the mall. Everywhere, and all of them had praised you. Talked about how a great personality you were. Mothers wished their sons were like you, and strangers wished they were a part of your life. They said they didn't think kind,good people existed in this era until they met you. They all said you were the epitome of comfort.They talked about your smile. A smile to die for. They wished you well and sent an overwhelming amount of condolences. They said they were sorry and happy all the same.Sad that it ended tragically and happy that you are in a better place now.

What saddens me the most is the part where I will be mentioning "you" and "was" in the same sentence. It will be better not to say anything at all, but to look for the brightest star in the constellation and keep an eye on it so it doesn't disappear on me. It guides me. Shines on me. Smiles on me. Like yesterday and always. You will forever be engraved in our hearts.

6

DEAR TEACHER

"Will I ever be your favorite student too?" Marang, 9 years.

I don't see the point of coming to school if none of my teachers believe in me. I believe that will bring the best out of me. Honestly, what would be the point of waking up at 5 a.m. every day only to be surrounded by people who don't believe in me? I want to be praised too, I want somebody to say, "I know you get nothing in class but trust me, if you put extra effort, you will get there. You know what makes the best students the best? Praise, and when everyone believes in them—that brings the best out of them. I want to be given chances too, not to be denied opportunities just because I am not brilliant, you all say. Yes, I understand why everyone, even the janitor, believes in a brilliant child and why they are always a top priority, but I am like them too. The god in them is still the god in me! I want to be given the same opportunities too, be it fairs, sports, academics, etc. I don't want to hear, "Mrs James, are you sure you are not going to disgrace yourself with the horse you chose to represent you?" anymore. If I want to try too, let me try instead of doubting me.

What about my poverty? I know I am poor but you cannot blame me for that; I didn't choose to be born poor and I am not going to let poverty come out of me. Do I merit being mistreated because of my social standing? Because I am poor? Because my mother is poor? Because our family is poor? But why? Am I the first person to be poor in this country? Can't the poor go to school freely and enjoy their school days just like any other? I know I come with an empty stomach but it doesn't make me any different from a kid who had cornflakes,sausages—what makes us different if we still have the same body cells, tissues, and systems operating merely the same? Our only difference here is that I am at risk of getting kwashiorkor (I would scream if I ever got that) while the kid who eats anything he wants might end up with obesity (damn, I hope they don't get that; obesity is scary).

However, I'll have you know that I'm also ravenous for knowledge: achieving outstanding academic success and getting a good education. Although I am impoverished, don't instantly assume that I will automatically perform poorly, because I try hard too. To get good grades. To be applauded. Appreciated for my improvements, little achievements.

I know you really don't like me one bit, but please understand that I am also making an effort to like you, your subject, the fucked-up educational system, my schoolmates, the school food, and the school in general. I'm really trying, but if you don't teach me anything and just pick on me constantly, it won't end well. Since I am a fellow human being too and am capable of extreme hatred, let's collaborate now while there is still time. I don't want either of us to look back and regret this.

P.S."Could you snap some pictures of me with your phone, like you did for everyone else?"

7

CERTIFIED LOSER

"Living will be more painful than dying but we should survive anywhere." Unknown.

A certified loser. That's what my colleagues called me. It's a moniker I've had since kindergarten and until the end of time, I was still a certified loser. Not merely a loser but a certified one! I had hoped for something better when I got accepted into the most prestigious college in the country, University of Botswana, UB.

I have lived all my school days barely enduring the label of a "certified loser" who was incapable of doing anything well. I had clumsy hands that occasionally slipped on everything they touched, causing me to make a lot of mistakes, and I got bullied for that. I would say I got used to being called names since I stepped into pre-school. It hurt at first but I got accustomed to the name-calling, the bullying, and just everything unpleasant that came with it.

Even though I put a lot of effort into everything I did, in their eyes, it was nothing, and I guess they never really paid much attention. Nobody wanted to sit next to me in kindergarten. Kids said my hands were sloppy and I stank. I also had no friends in my primary school days because they said my hands were clumsy and they didn't need anyone like me beside them either. My high school days were horrible too; they told me my stomach was always growling, and to save them from the tiger in my stomach, I should stay away from them at all cost.

The moment I laid my eyes on the faces in my new class, in college, I recognized innocent, fresh faces—no faces from any of my former schools—and I assumed I was free from all the insults. I was relieved that no one knew me and that I would no longer be referred to as a certified loser. I had let out a sigh of relief and silently thanked the heavens. I had no idea the same fate awaited me. They abruptly decided they didn't want anything to do with me. To my exclusion, they would huddle in small groups and chat excitedly among themselves. They formed a gang without me and would go out to parties together. They would choose their friends to work with on assignments and take-homes and they never chose me. The time the lecturer had created groups herself, guess what they did? They disbanded and joined different groups, leaving me on my own to conduct extensive research, write an analysis, design presentation slides, and deliver the entire lecture.

"Why would we stay in a group with her? I don't like her sense of fashion. Second, I don't like that pathetic face of hers. She is a total loser."

"She is so clueless about what is going on, look at her . . ."

"Nothing good comes from being close with her."

They had driven me to the point that I stopped trying.

"Do you have any friends?" the lecturer had asked after calling me to her office the other day.

"No, I don't have one."

"What kind of a person doesn't have a friend?" she had inquired.

"No one wants to be friends with a loser. They would gain nothing," I had answered.

"And guess what? You won't make it in this life without someone who challenges and encourages you to work hard. Before you quit on your own, you are going to fail miserably and you will be thrown in the streets . . . loser."

She had spat in my face—told me I wouldn't amount to anything in life and I was going to fail miserably. I dragged my feet, lifelessly, out of her office. She had also called me a loser. I plopped down on the bed when I got to the dormitory I shared with "Little Ms. Michael Jackson Style" and debated with one hell of a thought: Should I just quit this whole school thing because nothing was working out? I worked all alone most of the time and I would not understand a lot of things all alone, hence I would always get the minimum pass mark and nothing more. My parents would flip out and burn this entire planet if

I mentioned the word "quit." Maybe I should work extra hard, pull all-night studies, and study until there was nothing left of me. I came to that conclusion.

"Yes, studying and studying and that is how I will pull through."

That was the beginning of madness. I studied all the time and I would read and research until my blood ran cold. And it paid off. I had passed all my modules when the semester came to an end. My instructors would trust in me because I now had 60s and 70s, which indicated that with more work, I could obtain 80s and 90s.

I no longer cared if I completed an assignment by myself or with someone to whom they had also given the cold shoulder. I had no interest in anything. All that counted was finishing school, earning a degree, and landing a job. And in fact, I graduated with a pretty high GPA. Shortly afterward, I had begun looking for a job. I applied to different organizations and waited and waited, while I checked my emails and nothing came. I never gave up. I kept applying for jobs in my field, and with my qualifications, I thought I was a big deal—only to realize that wasn't the case at all.

I was stuck at home doing nothing for almost an entire year, and my parents got tired of taking care of someone who studied for six years in a school they never had the privilege to go to and who, on top of that, had a degree; what other kids her age would kill to have.They kicked me out of their house, and I was on the streets for a week before I coincidentally ran into my ex, with whom I was not on good terms. I begged him to take me in while

I was still figuring out my life. He told me he had a girlfriend but would take me in anyway.

"High risk, high returns," he'd said with a sly smirk.

What was that supposed to mean? I didn't know. He allowed me to move into his place in return for sex, as I learnt later. I had no choice anyway but to agree to his terms. Fourteen years later, I am still stuck in his apartment, sleeping with him all he wants and living off him like a real certified loser!

8

THE LAB RAT

"In the end, we are all lab rats." Masego, 34 years.

Dear Motswana-Woman, make me unknown. No . . . I am the lab rat . . .

THE MOMENT HE STEPPED INTO MY LIFE, MY WORLD WAS LIT ON FIRE. A second ago, I had made up my mind—I'd finally decided to become celibate and, now, a second later, metaphorically speaking, I'd become a whole princess irrevocably in love, and when another second went by, I'd become a lab rat.

I had loved everything about Thabo. He was the rare gem I had been searching for my whole life. I'd believed the universe had worked overtime in bringing us together. I never regretted a single moment I spent with him. His honey-kissed eyes sparkled whenever I was nestled in his arms. He smiled into my whole world, lighting it up like a Christmas bulb, and from the moment he stepped into my life, it has always been nothing but blissful moments. And my life never darkened again. I'd swear his muscles scared all the demons that neared me. He'd kiss me softly on my forehead and whisper nothing but seductive endearments that drove me off the deep end. I was crazed.

"You are my forever, princess," he whispered into my ears every night before he'd cuddle behind me and wrap his arms around me ever so protectively. I'd thought I'd met God in human form. He was my everything, the beginning and the end! He was the true definition of love. His love was so pure and genuine, I felt content and independent of anything or anyone. I even cut off my childhood best friend of fifteen years. He had filled my heart until it overflowed in a matter of seconds

And I couldn't thank God enough for bringing him into my life; he was the only source of light in my gloomy and hopeless life. All my relationships had failed miserably, never lasting longer than three days. Pathetic right? Love songs were not relatable at all. They meant nothing to me. All that mattered were sad songs. They knew my matters more than I did. I'd dated assholes my whole, entire life, and I had already seen my future self—old, haggard, senile, and no one by my side, only black cats, and I would be renowned as the village witch. But change of events: I will no longer be surrounded by cats anymore. I will be with Thabo and our four lovable babies. Beautiful kids with brown eyes who will be very kind and gentle, like Thabo.

I think I have always been a sucker for relationships. I'd dated boys from all the tribes there are in our country. I would move from Tswana to Herero to Kalanga to San and still nothing. At the end of the day, we would only tear each other into shreds until there was nothing left of us. The word "love" tasted like poison in my buds and every time somebody mentioned it, I would scrunch my face in disgust and ask, "What do you mean? What do you want from me?" Because nobody ever really loved me. And at the end of the day, I would believe in their lies and fall for their tricks. I would try to be there all the time. I would open my legs wholeheartedly and yet still they would leave the next day.

What could be wrong with me as a woman?

I had wondered all my life.

And I'd realized I was nothing to anyone. My father was never there in the first place and my mom left too, when I was little. She'd said, "I'll be back after I have gathered my life together," and that was the last time I saw her. Everybody else who has come into my life, they all left the next day. Being lovesick, as I was, I fell for every twisted lie and did my best to feel needed. I would clean their house, do laundry, and cook . . . I would paint their house and sell my body to bring as much money as I could. Once I got tired and decided to start adopting cats, the planets shifted to my favor.

"Hey. I am the new tenant and I will be staying across the hall," Thabo had said after a soft knock. I stood there, lost in his entrancing tawny eyes and husky voice.

"You look nice . . . I meant nice to meet you," I'd said shyly, blushing at the handsome new tenant. My stomach had back-flipped twice already. My palms sweated and I shook his hand vigorously. His hand was so soft and I would swear to god, this dude had been hiding all his life, taking care of his hands.

"I love your hands," I had muttered under my breath, and he'd just smiled and said, "I love you too." AND THAT WAS THE FIRST RED FLAG I'D IGNORED . . .

From that moment, I couldn't hide my excitement whenever I bumped into him across the hall. I would peek at him through the window and do absolutely anything that would get his attention. And every time he smiled, my heart would squirm and butterflies would dance in the pit of my stomach. He would listen to every word I uttered intently, and always knew when to chirp in. He took care of me and would protect me all the time, and my heart grew fonder . . . until one day I woke up in his arms. Things had escalated really quickly between us. He just turned and leaned to kiss me, his honey eyes sparkling like the edges of refined diamonds. My body just melted to his soft lips that were pressed against mine.

"I love you." He looked into my eyes and captured my lips for the second time.

Tears started welling in my eyes. I couldn't hide how happy I was. I would kill for the entire tribe because of this boy. He had filled me with nothing but an immeasurable amount of hope, love, and dreams. Five days of dating him felt like eons. And I listened to a thousand love songs overnight because I could relate now. I had started journaling my everyday life with him, not forgetting to come up with our babies' names—Ryan, Reign, Ronaldo, and Raymond. . . and I went on and created our couple page on Facebook: T-MASH couple. We were determined to take down the Riss-Quan. Their time was over. I mean, "I" was determined. After unblocking all my thirty-two exes to tell them I was getting married, I gathered everyone and told them to start downloading wedding songs and practicing wedding dances.

"I will love you till infinity . . ." he'd said as he lifted his heavy body off me.

"Why did you turn off your lights today?"

"Feels hot in here," he'd answered tersely.

Silence filled the pitch-dark room as I awkwardly laid on top of his bed, naked.

"Can you sleep in your room tonight? I want to be alone."

I hesitated for a minute, before I slunk to my feet and grabbed my clothes from the floor. I was disappointed in him and, thanks to the darkness, he wouldn't be seeing how disappointed I was. I waited at the door for him to hug me, kiss me goodnight, and walk me to my door.

"Hey, sleep tight," he breathed.

With that, he closed his door and I stood there like a lost puppy. I felt a lump form in my throat. Just when I took a step towards the direction of my room, I heard murmurings and a laugh followed.

"You got nerve, babe . . . She stinks . . . and don't forget to change the sheets."

I turned in slow motion like I was a movie character, as real-isation hit me like a wave. Instantaneously, his bulb flicked on.

"I've vomited multiple times and scrubbed my lips with deter-gent. Now, I must let her know, there was never a thing between us."

I took another step, something that seemed impossible. My feet and eyelids were so heavy. Everything became so heavy. Fighting the tears that were falling uncontrollably, I took another step. My whole world was curving in and crumbling before my eyes. I'd never asked Thabo if he was seeing anyone before I dived into him like a food-deprived lion. When I looked back, it had always been me talking about the future, talking about "us," and always trying way too hard to make the relationship work.

"She stinks."

Her syrupy voice echoed in my ears.

I just plopped into my bed. I remembered how I broke up with my first boyfriend. Nothing was working and he didn't give a damn about it and I always looked so pathetic, trying to save a relationship that was no longer there, so I just stopped trying at all and it ended just like that.

My second boyfriend had said, "Go, you deserve better."

My third boyfriend had just woken up that day and said that the world was such a big ocean, with plenty of fish.

My fourth boyfriend's niece I was tutoring turned out to be his daughter and her mother was back in town. He left for the mother of his child.

And as we go down the list, it becomes terrible and unbearable.

"He is different from all of them and he is not like any other." I spent the entire night turning and twisting in bed, assuring myself over and over again. When morning came, I hadn't slept a wink. I battled with every cell in my body to stop the tears from falling as I stared at the white ceiling. I heard a faint knock. I stumbled to the door and threw it open and to my surprise, Thabo stood at my door. His lips curled into a little smile that vanished in a split second as his honey-kissed eyes grew dark with venom and contempt. He handed me some paper and a pen before turning around and returning to his room.

"Let's just end it here. We were never going to get married anyway."

That was the sentence written on the paper in black ink.

"What do you mean?"

I dived into the writing competition too. I trudged across the hallway to his room and gave it to him.

"I mean you were never my type in the first place. It was just an experiment."

As my eyes fell on each syllable, my throat became increasingly parched. I forced a strong swallow, but there was no saliva in my mouth at all. As I grabbed the paper in my fist and nearly crumbled it into a small ball, my eyes quickly blinked.

"An experiment?"

I questioned.

"Yes. It was my 'real' girlfriend's idea."

THE EXPERIMENT HAS COME TO AN END.

I looked at the line in disbelief. What about us? What about the genuine love I saw in his eyes? What about your pure intentions? What happened to "until infinity?" Did infinity mean today? How come it had arrived so soon?

I was going insane. I reached for the refrigerator, yanked open the door, and stuck my head inside while still holding the door. My brain was burning to ashes in my head and my heart was numb. The cold breeze from the refrigerator wasn't helping, hence I grabbed ice blocks, planted them on my head, and wrapped a towel around my head. The next day, I woke up in a Psychiatry unit, surrounded by weird people calling me "trial and error." My whole body was covered in a very white bandage and my body burned like I was in hell.

NOW, I KNOW WHY HE HAD LIT THE MATCH! TO FINISH OFF THE RAT AFTER THE EXPERIMENT.

9

I HATE YOU, I LOVE YOU.

"It sucks to be you, Dad." Maria, 16.

Growing up, I never understood why my mother despised me so much until I met you, and now I know. I reminded her of a liar, a callous good-for-nothing who not only broke her heart but crushed and crushed it until there was literally nothing left of it. Since you are the kind to never keep your promises, I bet you did the same to her. Promised her stars, oceans, and the galaxy, only to give her a lifetime of heartbreak! I thought that a real man kept his promises. I thought that a true man protects what he cherishes. I thought that a real man would go to any length to protect his family, but thanks to you, I now seem delusional. You are completely the opposite of what I'd expected and all I did was keep assuring and reassuring myself, "He will do better. He is human after all."

Why did I believe such?

You were never there to begin with! You tossed my mother aside like a disposable vape and changed places, moved in with your new *"very adorable"* family which contained a bunch of headless idiots, starting with your new wife.

Thanks to you, who showed off your fertility and left, I had to grow up in a very toxic environment. I had to be reminded every day that I was born out of wedlock. I had to be reminded that my father didn't provide for me. I had to be reminded every day that I was the daughter of someone who was yet to be hunted down, like you were some sort of a terrorist.

Why did you have to make my life so difficult? My mother hated me so much that, had she been able to, she would have killed me. But I would assert that she killed me a thousand times over with her words, and pushed me off of a cliff a million times with her looks. And let's talk about school—I became a target for bullies. They slandered me and reminded me that I wasn't a member of my family.

But then, almost out of nowhere, you seemed to care, which was a lie, out of remorse. When I first saw you, my heart surged with excitement since you resembled me remarkably. I had closed my eyes and given the universe praise for uniting us. You had a soothing voice and warm arms.

I'd believed I had finally met someone who would look out for me, provide for me, and make me feel better, but it was all a lie. You are never there when I wake up frantic from the terrors of the night. You are never there to lend me a shoulder or engulf me in your warm arms. All you did was utterly disappoint me from time to time. Break my heart and crush it entirely, with nonchalance.

Remember when I was in middle school? I had to be thrown out of school because you didn't pay for my tuition fees. I missed the middle school graduation party because you didn't even bother paying for my expenses or getting me clothes for the party. Because of you, I was unable to attend my late friend's funeral! I had to ask for toiletry donations every time the school term started since I was in a boarding school. You had promised to help, be there always, and make up for the difficult times I had to go through.

You never make an effort and I want you to know that I HATE YOU SO MUCH and I must tell you this: the year I land a decent job, I will reimburse you for all the money you have spent on me since we met, and we won't have the father-daughter relationship we almost had. No, we stop. Rewind. Erase. And reset back to when we didn't know each other. Yes, let's start there—before the hunting began.

I hope you protect the new family you love so much and invest in them immensely so that they never leave their sponsor, their bank, and they stick to you to the very end, like they are your blood, which they are not.

Ah, another time, I had teachers watching me like a hawk in high school after you decided to buy me the wrong colors of the uniform, and I was getting punished every day, attending classes uncomfortably while my classmates called me a transfer student for two years straight! I will never forget that. I will never forgive you either.

It is not like me to give someone more than one chance, but I gave you several chances to be better for me. I didn't expect a lot from you, you just had nothing to offer in the first place as my other parent. I wished you could keep your promises, I wished you were like other fathers. I wished you could keep my nightmares away. I wished you could have at least pretended to love me as your daughter to compensate for not being there for the whole of my life.

But since water has become thicker than blood, we can't reverse the damage! I am going to become the most successful person alive, and please refrain from pointing to the pictures in the newspapers claiming to know the big me. By that time, I would have drained all your blood that is in me and flushed it down the drain. Don't come looking for me and I will do the same. I hate you! *I love you.*

10

WHEN YOU REMEMBER ME

"Even when you feel like you are alone, don't throw yourself away." *Promise*, Park Jimin.

Dear real me,

"I am glad I still remember how you smile, even though I don't know who you are anymore. It is a pity I search for you, you who have always been with me since the beginning of time. I am so sorry to you. The smile I see in the mirror screams that I know you, but my heart—or is it my brain?—can't tell if I know you or if I claim to know you while I don't . . ."

When it began, I'd just brushed it off. A bad joke, I'd thought, and I took it lightly but now it feels so unbearably heavy, I can't just shove it off my shoulders that easily. It requires men with herculean muscles and big brain cells. At first, it was a simple bad appetite, and before I knew it, nothing made sense in my mouth.

We upgraded—or is it degraded?—to just wandering aimlessly as everything that was light, life, and love made no sense at all. My favourite songs, my favourite clothes, my ultimate favourite people, and everything became dull and uninteresting. I lost all interest. Movies made no sense. My comic books lay untouched. My hair overgrown. Packets of my snacks, which I once devoured like they were the elixir of life, were all opened and barely touched, all of them. My vigor had vanished. The weight of it made me wonder why I should continue living when I can just die. End my life. Fortunately, I stopped there. No attempts.

Do you know the most painful feeling in the entire universe? It is feeling empty. When you feel an insurmountable void swirling inside of you. An abyss of emptiness that nothing can fill up, not even hefty carats of diamonds and gold. I'd swear, it beats them all. It is the real devil. I would not know what exactly I wanted. I'd do this and that and at the end of the day, nothing made sense no matter what I did.

From time to time, all I did was wonder what level of sorcery this was, and I'd wrack my brain insanely to get answers. I would think of everything all at once. All things popping open like popcorn. I spiraled. It was painful. My brain. I shook my head rapidly to shake the pain off. I banged my head on the wall to stop it from the exhaustive non-stop processing, but all I got was a hard, protruding horn on my forehead. It was sick. I ended up contemplating destiny. What if I was not living rightly? What if God was punishing me for deviating from my divinely destined path?

Like seriously, what do I know about destiny? I am only a child. Who doesn't even know who he is or what he is capable of? I just slept. But when I thought it would become my escape, that too became a luxury I could not afford. I twisted and turned every night and everyone I met mistook me for a panda- dark circles around my eyes. When my friends asked me what was going on, I'd told them it was just a phase. It would pass. I'd assured them not to worry about me. I'd made sure my face stayed as neutral as water as I answered them since, in all honesty, I had no idea what was going on. I was just as clueless and as eager for an answer as they were.

When night fell, I lay awake as my brain shifted from this to that like an ADHD kid. Digging and retrieving things from the Before Christ era, mixing with the present, making plans for the future, resurrecting dead, buried, bad emotions, and kept on repeating the present and changing scenarios from better to worse and vice versa.

I heaved up from my bed and trudged swiftly to my bookshelf, which was barely standing on its own thanks to my collection of comics. It was by God's grace this shelf was still standing! I grabbed volume one of *Demon Slayer* and eyed the other volumes before I leapt onto my bed with it. I searched for the fortitude to open it and found a little, but when I was three pages away from the end, I was bored as fuck and wanted to try a different volume. I stood back up, went over to shelf again, and grabbed a different volume. Yet another volume. One more, a different volume. Why was it so hard to read like before? I'd sighed like a poisoned chameleon before I furiously threw them across the room.

I ate this and that until my stomach was upset and ached. That was when I started crying, not because of the pain in my stomach but because I didn't know how I was going to help myself. How long it was going to take, and most importantly, how I'd save myself. What if I was going to be like this forever? I bawled my eyes out until they felt void from crying.

I was hopeless.

I was not going to be okay again.

I was void.

But I had to save myself no matter what because nobody was coming to save me. I grabbed a piece of paper and wrote a letter to the real me. I made sure to include the things I loved to do, my favorite cuisines, my favorite music, and everything else that was a part of me. Not just a part of me, but I. The places I'd visited with my friends. I rewrote my dreams, found my inspirations again, and when I was done finding the real me, I folded it nicely and whispered softly into it, "*When you remember me, call me and I will come running to you, you who is me and only the real I.*" It bloomed into a flower. The flower I have always been.

11

MONNAMOGOLO

"Just living, and caring less, would suffice." Headhunter101.

I heard that I was born the same day my great grandfather passed and that was how I ended up inheriting his name. When I was a little kid, I would sprint when somebody yelled "Monnamogolo." I thought it was a popular name, only to find out that the name refers to "old man." Old man was my stupid name—it was like the title of a cliche Korean drama that starred a demented, old, toothless hag who was there to tell the Gen Alphas endless, boring, Joseon-era stories.

When the old man kicked the bucket, he'd left a wish and that was to name the first male great-grandson to be born following his passing after him. My parents being my parents, they honored the elderly man's request and never even thought of giving me a second name or making Monnamogolo a second. I could have been Ezra, Thabo, Mickey, Austin, Karabo, or Mariam, for Pete's sake! I mean, there are a lot of names to choose from and yet they stuck to Monnamogolo like their life depended on it, meanwhile it was my own life that depended on it like no other.

"*Tse di jang pension*," my teacher teased while he was handing us our test papers.

All the kids laughed in my direction. I just dragged my feet like an old man to where he was standing.

"Poor old man . . . I was about to bring the paper to you. You shouldn't have bothered. I would have brought your test paper, along with a cup of tea."

All the kids laughed like hyenas and made funny sounds.

Today, too, I will have to keep my cool and pretend I can't hear Mr. Elijah teasing me. Act as though I can't hear these idiots laughing at me, but trust me, if this keeps on happening, I am going to throw a tantrum at home and get my parents to change my name. I don't care if it was my great grandfather's; I want my own name, not that of someone else. I am afraid the next thing I will be told is to pursue his undiscovered potential or become a traditional doctor as he was.

I just dragged my feet back to my seat, which was not far from the chalkboard because I had bad eyes and my body was always tired. My eyes always drooping, heavy. An old man, exactly, I was. I was glad that my absolutely handsome face had no wrinkles.

"You can sleep now, old man," my classmate teased, and a boisterous laugh followed. The other students laughed too, again. I heard a laugh a day keeps the doctor away, but with these kids, it was extreme. A mental institution is where they were all supposed to be, not school.

I'd hoped everyone would have moved past making fun of my stupid name so far, since we had been in the same class since preschool and now we were in grade three. These kids were still the same—*talk about a man who's easier to take to Mars than to change.* I met horrible teachers like Mr. Elijah, who pulled horrible pranks on me all the time. My classmates became more like him every second they spent with him.

"Mom? Dad?"

"What? Do you have anything to say?" Mom enquired.

"Can't I have my name—?"

"Not happening."

She cut me off before I could finish.

"Your great grandfather wanted you to be named after him. He was a very great person and you are going to be just like him— great and extremely wise," she'd continued.

"But . . ."

"Don't sweat over it, sweetie. The folks who are continuously making fun of you will ultimately grow weary of it and will leave you alone."

She patted my head lightly.

I knew she wasn't going to listen to me, and I had thought maybe Dad would agree with me or at least say something, but he remained quiet, never daring to open his mouth, as if he was told, "Just stay quiet. I will handle this."

I dragged my sore feet to my bedroom. My knees were painful. Osteoarthritis? Jesus, I was still young. I wouldn't get arthritis because of this stupid name, right? I plopped into bed and stared blankly at the nicely designed, thatched roofing. I just stared at the point where those poles met until an idea popped into my mind.

I left for school very early and immediately when I arrived, I collected all my books—every book that had my name, from where books were stacked nicely according to different subjects. I turned the brown covers inside out, went to the teacher's desk, grabbed a green permanent marker, and started writing all my books.

Mo-a-ne-lwa-mo-go-lo.

Yes, that would be my new name. I could become the main character, not an old man anymore. It made me feel like some old piece of shit. Being the main character was not bad, right? But Mr. Elijah and my classmates were very unpredictable. They might never stop teasing me. It might become much worse. What would I do?

I would change my name to Elijah or one of my colleagues'!

Simple stuff. I was done with this stupid name.

"Monnamogolo," the teacher said while looking at my book. I just kept quiet and went ahead to collect my book. I know she feigned blindness.

"Monna . . . mogolo," Ms. Gomolemo said.

I just padded to where she was standing and grabbed my book from her hands and shuffled back to my seat.

"Attitude, grandpa," she remarked, not looking in my direction, her hands grabbing another book and calling the next student.

"Mo . . . A . . ." Mr. Dennis paused. "Moanelwa . . . No . . . No . . . What am I seeing? Monnamogolo, come over here. When did your name change?" he questioned.

"Yesterday," I said nonchalantly and beamed.

"Big guy. Now, you are the main character."

He gave me a high five.

"Yes, sir."

I smiled briefly before he threw the book at my face.

"Don't fool around, Monnamogolo. Turn that cover now!"

I literally heard my stomach drop to my feet. I was doomed! The moment I turned this cover inside out, I would be doomed. I would have to turn all the book covers inside out. All of them. Back to old man.

"I changed my name so I am not going to turn this cover inside out!" I emphasized firmly.

"Okay, big guy. Do whatever you want; I don't care whether you are some senile man or the main character!"

With that, he grabbed the next book and yelled louder than before,

"Lesedi!"

"My-mo-na-mogolo." Our English teacher, an old foreign woman, said as usual, with an accent.

"That's not my name. It is Moanelwamogolo, which translates to main character," I corrected her. She was sweet and always called me her Monnamogolo. I never corrected her. She was a widow.

"Ohh, now you have become the main character. I like the name."

She smiled sweetly before she gave me my book. I felt my heart squirm for the first time. I felt a little happy.

"Monnamogolo!" the last period teacher screamed at the top of her lungs. I know why she was behaving like a crack donkey. She wanted to get done with giving us our books, throw us another exercise, and be gone right away.

"Easy, chewing gum machine," someone at the back said.

Everyone, we found when we came for grade one, called her chewing gum machine and we never got her real name.

"Chewy . . . I am no longer Monnamogolo. You read it all wrong."

"Good luck with your new name, buddy, I got to be somewhere."

With that, she yelled the last name and left the classroom instantly.

I tried to change my name for the past seven years, but I was still Monnamogolo. Once a potato, always a potato! My classmates called me grandpa and they were always pestering me to tell them stories about World War II and colonization, which I wasn't there. They would bring me a warm cup of coffee now and then and encourage me to sleep in class. Surprisingly, this name worked to my advantage and these kids never hated the name. They said it was a unique name and they would die to be named after their grandparents too, and they'd loved it since the very first time they heard it.

"My name is—"

"We already know who you are. Sit down."

My name had reached places I had never been to!

I jumped and screamed. The judges of the competition I'd joined threw me a look. I ran outside, screaming and whooping.

12

RICH TALK

"Stay away from places you don't belong." Head-
hunter101.

I couldn't so much as lift my feet off the ground. I was
wasted. Wasted to the last number and the garrulous
strangers surrounding me wouldn't stop talking. They
had been this way, since . . . sin . . . ce way before the
invention of alcohol. Way before 7000 BCE, in China
where residues in clay pots revealed the guys capable of
absolutely anything were making alcoholic beverages
from rice and millet. Wouldn't shock me into a coma
if they made Jesus from scratch and brought him to
this world, so they could nail him again—his cousins?
Roman soldiers?

It was just a lot of them. I couldn't count with my head spinning like a Ferris wheel and my eyes in such a hazy state. But I swear to God, nobody blabs nonsense like a kid who has rich parents and has traveled to whatever country. They left me speechless. I gulped down the content of the glass I was holding. It burnt my throat. A refill, by whoever I couldn't make out, his face blurry. Another gulp. Another refill. And it went on and on until the last thing I heard was the voice of the round girl with plump, rosy cheeks reverberating in my head. Playing and replaying over and over again. She was telling this group of lads that in the United States, the house they stay in was once Nicki Minaj's home. They all gaped at her with sheer interest, awestruck. I had just blacked out on the large couch occupying the vast room, crawling with tipsy, high teenagers.

I said a short prayer, curtly. I was now free from being made insecure, my poverty rubbed in my face constantly, and being reminded I hadn't boarded a plane in my life yet. Rich kids were so boastful, it was exhilarating! How I ended up here, it was uncanny. A friend I had met through a friend who I had met through a friend called in sick at work and out of the goodness of my heart, I'd bought a basket full of fruits and flowers and dropped by where she stayed.

I had left the compound after seeing her. She was walking me to the bus stop when a luxurious car sped up and drenched us with water that had accumulated in ditches on the gravel road. The driver then slowed down to apologize. I had no idea who I would see in that car when the window rolled down. It was Letlhogonolo, a guy who was formerly regarded as my best friend by the entire school. He was driving the newest Jeep, with tinted glasses like he was the mayor in his own city. The last time I saw him was on our final day of middle school, graduation day.

"Catch you on the next train." Those were his last words before we parted in high school.

The next train came, and he was not there. Now he came up in a Jeep, forgetting he had promised to board the next train with me. I looked at him in disbelief after he said, "Sorry, kids."

Sorry, kids? I had repeated in utter disbelief. How was this guy here, with a beard and a deep voice calling women kids? For fuck's sake, I must have been mistaken—Letlhogonolo was a respectable kid. He apologized. I let it slide. After he passed, he stopped momentarily and asked if I knew or was related to a certain kid he knew who went by the name Mandy.

"Mandy who?"

"Mandy Maungomantle?"

"I am Mandy. I thought I mistook you for Letlhogonolo. You are the Letlhogonolo I know of, right?"

"Oh yeah, babes. Jump in, so we can catch up."

It was so hard to believe this was the Letlhogonolo I'd met in middle school. Babes? What happened to that innocent kid? Curiosity got the best of me and my feet did things my brain could have never conjured up. Tracy, my coworker, and I jumped into his car. He stayed in the walled house just adjoining the walls of where Tracy lived. What a small world, I'd thought quietly because never in a million years did I think one day I would bump into Letlhogonolo just after closing Tracy's gate.

"Where you work at?"

"The Brains Law Firm."

"Whoa, you did become an attorney?"

"Yeah, well, I am an intern there."

I didn't even bother asking him where he worked and stuff because it was very clear he had a job that paid far better than mine.

He plucked out something from the glove compartment. It was a small remote. He pressed it and the huge gate slid open. As it slid open, we heard noise, chattering and music playing softly in the big white house packed with rich kids. They smoked weed, drank very expensive alcohol, wore expensive sneakers, and I was there with my friend wearing flip flops from Pep Stores.

These presumptuous kids talked incessantly about their parents' money and told us they did all the things that we, poor kids without rich parents, thought were impossible. We tried fitting in for eons and I realized, you can't force a chicken to walk like a dog when it hasn't got four legs—I don't know if you get it but nevertheless that is how I ended up drinking alcohol like a possessed spirit and collapsing into the nearest sofa. When I woke up the next day, I made a mental note not to ever hang out with rich kids again.

13

FUCKED UP

"If I can have Bale, why not you too?." Melody, 36.

I AM SO FUCKED! I exhaled loudly like a madman for the hundredth time. If not the hundredth, it must have been the thousandth time now. My colleague kept on asking what was wrong and all I could do was exhale loudly. I just didn't know where to start, or what to tell him exactly, because his prophecy had come to pass.

I had thought of dragging him to a far, far corner the same way he had dragged me the other time to warn me not to fall for the new guy's enchanting smile. He'd told me to dash whenever I heard his name. The next thing I knew, we met in the kitchen, and he'd jutted his hand in my direction with a "Nice to meet you, I am Khalid." I'd vigorously wiped my hand on my skirt and shook his with an "I can't imagine my life without you too."

I had known my three brain cells would throw me under a bus

sooner or later, and I wasn't shocked when they did. He'd smiled deviously anyway and whispered *I will call you later* sexily before he disappeared around the corner without witnessing the butter he was leaving behind melt.

We had bumped into each other multiple times. Most of the time, I was leaving the kitchen and him the opposite. He would drag me back into the kitchen to keep him company while the coffee brewed, the milk warming. My heart warming. Feelings brewing. Another one of my colleagues warned me too. I don't remember how many other people warned me not to fall for his treacherous tricks.

I, now, blame the animal in my uterus. He must have come with amnesia. So, his friend was the first person to warn me. He told me he was a typical playboy, a babe magnet who always gets what he wants and is never serious with anyone. I brushed him off—he must be a jealous friend, I thought and had responded with a, "*Nako ke yone e seyong nnake.*" I am not a cat that has nine lives. Not even a day had passed and I'd known of his ill intentions. A hit and run, they called it in the black market, but who was I to resist a whole red flag in front of me? I loved red flags.

I didn't care whether we had nothing in common at all. I didn't care whether he flirted with another girl in my vicinity, or they slept together. Who would steal my match from heaven? They couldn't steal someone else's soulmate, could they? After a week with him, I'd learnt he had a girlfriend who was working in the UK. It was a twelve-year relationship that even thousands and thousands of kilometers wouldn't end, and here I was, way out of his league and thinking he would stay. He would stick with me. I hoped he stuck around. I had learned genies who supposedly grant wishes didn't exist. Or if they existed, they were in a deep slumber when I needed them.

We only talked when he was in the mood to talk to me. He only babied me when we were being intimate. We did things when he was in the mood and did them the way he wanted. I visited and slept over at his place when he was in the mood or too generous that day. I was practically alone in that relationship. I sailed the ship on my own. It wasn't tiring though, because for a minute I had believed I might have saved my country in my past life. I had thought I deserved somebody this good looking for the sake of my kids, hence ignored the general danger signs and ended up fucked.

When I told him I was pregnant with his child, he'd congratulated me nonchalantly. He turned the tables on me and told me I approached him and seduced him, so he gave me good-looking kids and said he was going to leave since he had fulfilled my wish. He even invited me to his wedding, which was to take place in a few days, without forgetting to rub it in my face that he was marrying the woman of his dreams. I pretended not to give a damn. I had a well-paying job anyway—who was he kidding? I could support myself, this damn baby, and give him the best life that every kid dreams of.

But after nine months of carrying Bale, I realized I must have betrayed my country in my past life—he was a replica of somebody I now loathed with every cell in my body, the very person I was striving to delete with every fiber of my being. To forget completely, and I was failing miserably. The deadpan. The dominance oozed like he was the baby crown prince. And with him looking like this, like Khalid, I was fucked up big time. How was I supposed to carry on? Pretend I was okay when in reality, I wasn't? I knew we had a relationship that lasted a blink of an eye but what was I going to do if I loved him so much? If I had fallen too deep and could not live without him. With Bale being the constant reminder of him, how was I supposed to not cry every day?

I had men asking me out from time to time. I turned them down because all the damn time, I would search for Khalid in them, and when I realized they weren't Khalid, I wouldn't even listen to them. For the rest of my life, I wanted Khalid and no one else. For my entire life, I had looked at Bale painfully while I pondered one and the same thing over and over again: "If I can have Bale, why can't I have you too?"

14

WHEN THE MUSIC STOP

"In my next life, don't take my life away." Botshelo, 13.

When you are homeless, people treat you like a fucking stone. They bump into you and never say sorry, step on you and don't show even a slight sign of remorse. They treat you like you are a mere obstacle, insignificant and forgotten. But again, the only people who matter in this world are the people who have a place called home. I don't have such a place, yet the voices in the fucking headphones promise to take me anywhere, to the end of the world and back, and I really hope somewhere between the back, middle, and end, I will land in a place called home too.

I adjust my headphones before taking a seat beside an old woman. She gives me a toothless smile, and drool descends like fallen angels on her polka dot blouse. She wipes it away rapidly, while everyone on the bus literally makes disgusted faces. I turn on my music player and play songs loudly in my ears. They won't stop staring; they won't stop stepping on my toes. I want to shout and tell them having these headphones on does not mean I can't feel pain, smell, or see. But I can't. Because I would be labeled a deranged beggar. Not only a homeless kid anymore, but deranged too, and I might fucking wake up in a mental institution. I keep quiet and focus on the music, the beats, the lyrics, and everything that will numb the pain, the past, and the present.

When I have my headphones on, my demons forget I exist. They stop pestering me, torturing me, demanding anything from me. I would say they completely forget Botshelo. Or perhaps Life doesn't exist—that is what my fucking name translates to; Life. I never got to know why my mother named me Life because immediately after she gave birth to one, she took another away—hers.

I didn't know how I could have reacted if I wasn't just a baby then. But now, I look up at the vast sky above and silently ask, "Why did you leave so early? Why did you abandon me? What did I ever do to you?" Yet, there is no answer—just the vast expanse of silence above.

I heard I had a father. I don't remember him. I don't remember much, what he looked like. But I hear I'm the spitting image of only him and nobody else. I heard he couldn't take the news of my mother taking her life away. He went on to drink the remaining pieces of his life away and drove recklessly until he was found in a ditch somewhere, lifeless. He had hit a truck, lost control of the wheel, and the car went on to hit a tree, and was crushed to the size of a cup before it rolled into a nearby ditch.

Only one person made it out alive from "the car of a man who went on a suicide mission with his son," as the newspapers put it. I still have the paper with me, and from time to time, I ask the man who made it to the front page overnight: Did he really want to drag his innocent son to the pits of hell with him? That was so selfish of him. But who am I to judge a man who had lost the woman who gave him a reason to live? He was wrecked. Albeit I understand that part, I still can't find a reason why someone will not live for me.

The only luxury I ever had was my grandparents. I had both my maternal grandparents and a grandmother from my paternal side. I stayed with my maternal grandparents most of the time because my paternal grandmother couldn't stop calling me by her son's name with teary, unseeing eyes. I always reminded her who I was, but still, she went on incessantly, calling me "my baby, my baby." Her hands trembling violently as she patted the air, searching for my face. Until her last breath, she still reached out, calling me her son.

My maternal grandmother was exactly like my paternal grand-mother. She wandered around, following random strangers, calling them her daughter. We were always searching for her. One day, while we were searching for her, my diabetic grandfather collapsed and never woke up. If we could have been near his shots, perhaps he could have been saved. But unfortunately, we were not.

My maternal grandmother passed when I was in middle school— and just when I had thought maybe, just maybe, my life would become less hectic from running around like a lost puppy, my other relatives appeared. They came to scramble over the deceased properties and money she'd left and take away a place I'd called home for my entire life.

I ended up in the gutter, sharing crumbs of bread with rats. As I wandered around looking for a place I could call home, I met Robert, the well-known beggar who played an accordion in the heart of the city. He told me he had seen people from all walks of life, but he had never seen me before. "Not all who wander are lost," he said, "and nothing in this world cannot be fixed." He handed me an MP3 player and a pair of headphones, saying, "For while you wander." I reluctantly took them, my initial contempt fading away.

I walked around, the headphones on my ears, and suddenly people stopped talking about me everywhere I went. They didn't seem to notice me anymore. I couldn't hear my grandmother calling me "my baby." I couldn't hear the sound of the car crash. I barely remembered the route I used to take while I searched for my other grandmother. All I heard were angelic voices, an unending effort that had turned into beautiful pieces, hard work, and a very powerful force that is barely appreciated enough but can heal the sick, fix the broken, and bring back destiny. The strangers who knew how to express what I was going through without me having to tell them. I called them prophets, healers, and most of all my saviors. As the million voices shifted in the earpieces, I bawled my eyes out, both in public and in private.

When I take the headphones off, I see turmoil. I become sick. I feel lost. Life becomes meaningless, hopeless. My demons find their way back to me and I see a person hanging from a very tall tree—perhaps my mother. But when I approach that person, I realize it's my own body, lifeless.

It happened because they took my headphones away. Crashed my player. Took my music away. My life away. And now I am telling the story of my life from six feet underneath the ground. It feels peaceful though, like I am finally home.

I had an epiphany. Home was the million angelic voices that shifted in the earpieces.

That is when I knew I'd always been home.

15

HEADHUNTER101 QUOTE 1

"We are ignoring the people who genuinely care about us and giving attention to the people who don't give a single flying fuck and again, seeking the people we are ignoring in them. That is how we get hurt,used. So maybe, just maybe, give attention to the right people and stop expecting the wrong people to be the right people for you." Headhunter101.

16

DO I STOP NOW?

"Let me fall, fly." Kagiso, 43.

What do I do now? Find the perfect music to numb the pain? Cry my void to sleep? Try to make friends? What am I going to do with my head? It spirals in pain and now my neck feels like it's being eaten by snakes. The snakes in my dreams. The demons of my nights. Yet when I look closer, I realize they aren't the demons—I am the demon. How did I spend my entire life searching? To find purpose, to unravel the enigma of existence, to find a job, a lover, a father, happiness . . . Did I spend the rest of my life chasing shadows, hoping they would coalesce into something tangible? Chasing dust until the very end?

Right now, I stand on the edge of the ledge, and I wonder if there was anything to chase so relentlessly in the first place. Did I waste my entire life chasing nothing for nothing? What was the point of all the running, the trying, if I could have just sat and watched this life roll by? I didn't have to look for a mismatching symphony of fabrics, worn garments, and tattered coats to look like a beggar, I was already one. Born a beggar and dying a beggar. If and only if, I had realized that earlier, my life could have been much better. I could have just gotten myself a cardboard home, sat on street corners, found riches in the ordinary while I enjoyed life's scraps. Is it too late to do that now? But I have always turned right back, to do things better, to start fresh, only to end up at the same place, all over again. Hell.

One day I asked my friend, Lorraine, to be sober for the first time in history and give me proper advice but she repeated the same thing she had always said when she was drunk: "Stop trying too hard; there is literally nothing here to chase. Happiness? That is just an elusive butterfly that will flutter away every time you try to catch it, and money? Ah, the grand illusion! We chase it, believing it will unlock doors, yet often find ourselves trapped in gilded cages," and honestly, for a minute, I understood why she had spent her entire life drinking. She had chased the money, the happiness, the fame (she was an artist by the way) and knew when to stop, unlike me, who kept on chasing until I had no strength to stand on my own.

The last floor of a nine-floor building needed no strength at all. It was like being carried to the place where I belonged because I had been running to the wrong places. It felt like I belonged here. It felt like home for a minute. I looked at the cars below, the trees, and the people—they had turned smaller, like minions, and I was the giant yet insignificant person like I was on top of the world.

I had wanted to capture a memory of the below to take it to the underworld—to relish how it felt to be finally at the top and when everything had shrunk to a seed size. I saw the pieces of my life. When I had trudged endlessly from this door to that door looking for a job with a degree I had attained in a not very sweet way, because somebody said go to school, get good grades, go to university, and you will automatically get a job (education promised keys to any door) and yet every door I have been to has remained stubbornly shut. I had tried this business and that, but business has principles too, needs thorough research and needs the money that you are actually opening the business to make. Start-up capital and all that. I didn't know where to get that and now I think it would have been wiser to rob a bank.

I remember when I was young, and my mom had told me to work harder so my father would come back saying, "I am sorry I wasn't there for you when growing up, but I am your dad," and I would take him to one of his checkups in my Range Rover. But he has never come back, because I didn't get the Range Rover, and now I think I didn't work hard enough. My lecturer once said that too. That I don't work hard enough and I won't make it in life and I didn't.

At least I never went to prison, but what is the point when I went from that mental health facility to bigger ones and all I got were demons with cute names and hideous abbreviations like we were shooting a hit movie? Now I look back and I realize I never really understood it, when all that I tried doing said, "We would change your life, we will take you places one day." In fact, another world meant the underworld.

17

WHAT IS YOUR NAME?

"I really love you, Uncle Brendan . . . I heard she saved my life,
and in return, I am going to name my child after my savior."
Little Sion, 7.

The random fights we pick on Facebook nearly led to my doom
one day. Yet, through it all, I learned a few things, had someone's kid named after me, and even married someone I once
loathed with every bone in my body—Brendan. He was the kid
I met on Facebook. Being me, I left a provocative comment
under one of his posts and acted non-existent until he hunted
me down.

I left snarky comments, called him names, and posted offensive
remarks, knowing my accounts were fake and no one could find
out who I was or where I lived. I felt invincible, cyberbullying
kids who couldn't track me down. But Brendan was different.
He tracked me down and, being Brendan, also found my grandmother. I don't know how he discovered that she was the one I

had a special connection with.

It was around six forty-five p.m. when I visited my granny and learned that a scoundrel had broken her lock and stolen her phone. Only the phone was taken; everything else was untouched. I was fuming with rage. She wouldn't be able to call me every day until she got a new phone. She was the only person who called me, the only friend I had, the only human being interested in knowing about me. I went back to where I stayed with my mother and siblings. When I told them that someone had broken grandmother's lock just to steal a phone, I started suspecting the overly sensitive kid I messed with on Facebook.

Immediately, I logged into Facebook and found a new friend request from an account under my grandmother's name, with a profile picture of me. The pictures kept changing, different photos of me that were in my grandma's phone. After midnight, he started posting weird stuff. That's when I went into full detective mode to find him and maybe fight with him to get my granny's phone back. I got a friend of mine involved—he was good in IT. He tracked Brendan down to a bar and there he was, surrounded by some weird dudes. When I saw them, I turned around and pretended I wasn't pursuing him. He immediately sent me a text: "Don't be shy, come over here already." I nearly dropped my phone. How had he seen me? Now I suspected he had been stalking me for a while.

I stayed with my back turned, trying to muster up the rage that was there earlier, playing out fictional scenarios in my head. I figured Dutch courage would help, so I took Jägermeister shots before nearly going over to where he was seated. He had turned in my direction for a fraction of a second and that was enough to capture his beautiful complexion and the very handsome face he had—I just froze in my steps before I dashed. I didn't have time to call a ride. I was going to run all the way home, sleep with an axe beside me, and lock my room. Wake up every thirty minutes to check if the door was still intact.

I was almost home when a car suddenly appeared, speeding madly. It crashed into the sheltered waiting area and nearly caught fire. It was nearly engulfed in flames, but as if something—an unseen force—decided, "No! Not fire!" I heard a woman's voice cry, "Call 997!" and multiple baby cries. I frantically searched for my phone and called for an ambulance, literally in tears, begging them to arrive as soon as possible. The first baby had a hollow on the back of its head, blood oozing from the wound. The spinal cord had snapped in half. The other baby lay cold and still, and the third baby gave a chilling shriek. A woman's body, covered in blood, lay a few centimeters from the car. Three ambulances arrived, and that was when Brendan popped out of nowhere too.

Since then, we have always been at the hospital, watching an eleven-month-old baby turn into a seven-year-old so fast. The only survivor of that accident. All I did was sit there and listen to Brendan do most of the baby lessons—from teaching him to sit, feed himself, talk, and dress himself. I was just there, stealing glances when Brendan wasn't watching.

One day, we had a feud, and little Sion laughed so hard that day. Brendan was going to give all his childhood belongings to Sion—his favorite toys, his socks, just a lot of stuff—and I was totally against it. We went on and on until Sion said, "I really, really love you, Brendan. You are very handsome." And then, he turned to me and asked, "What is your name?" He had learned to say Brendan as his first word and had never heard my name since Brendan always called me "The Cyberbully-I-Caught-Red-Handed."

I told Sion my name-Zuri, and what the name meant His face lit up, he grabbed a piece of paper, scribbled it down, and said, "I am so sorry, Uncle Brendan. I am no longer going to name my child after you when I grow up and have kids, because I just heard a voice say she saved my life, and in return, I am going to name my kid after my savior."

Brendan nearly choked me to my demise upon hearing my name.

"Why didn't you ever tell me your name?" he asked.

"You never gave me the chance to," I replied.

"Whatever. I am marrying the girl with that name."

And that girl he was referring to, was me. He asked, *"Who did you think I was referring to when you are the only girl to ever exist with that name?"*

My grandmother had said, "Boy, you are going to pay for the lock you broke for the rest of your life . . ."

He'd smiled, his smile with a glitch and that is when I remembered the stories my grandmother and her friends always told
me. The ghost trains from the future that appeared at that bus
stop when it struck midnight. Race cars. Beautiful women
with hourglass bodies. Foreign men with manly voices and
mustaches. You will find beautiful babies cooing. Until they
start glitching and disappear, and you wake up from a ten-year
dream that unfolded in the span of a mere fifteen-minute nap."

18

LONELY, ASF.

"Just one friend: is it too much to ask, Universe?" Tshego, 22.

I feel empty, like there's nothing inside of me. When I'm with my friends, it's even worse, as if they've arrived carrying buckets of emptiness. Sometimes, I wonder if I'm really their friend or if that's just what I tell myself. They talk about themselves endlessly, never giving me a chance to share how I feel or what's happening in my life. It's always about them, as if the world revolves around their every whim.

They decide how I spend my student allowance, how I dress, and even the alcohol we drink when we're out partying. All dolled up like Barbie dolls, they command, "We're gonna be drinking Savanna all night, and you, get a box of Pulse too." They order me around without a second thought.

They talk about me right in front of me.

"My boyfriend wouldn't bat an eye in her direction, no matter how dolled up she is."

"She's a total frog in human form."

"And you know why my boyfriend wouldn't bat an eye in her direction? That hot guy always goes for chicks in his league, not some lowlife who only knows the smell of money thanks to university!"

The three of them would snort in unison and give each other high fives. Are they red flags, or am I over thinking? Why does it always feel like I'm throwing myself at them? Is there something wrong with me? Do I deserve to be treated like the princesses' servant? Was I? They had other friends who were more important to them than me. They only came to me when they wanted to borrow my last allowance to take their boyfriends out on dates, and when their "better-looking" friends were present, I wasn't invited.

When I realized that Loago, Maria, and Jacaranda were not the great friends I thought they would become, I found myself a new friend, Keolebogile. But unfortunately, she had friends she ran to all the time and that was when I thought, "I think I will do well on my own."

I stopped interacting with the three princesses and Keolebogile altogether. The fear of being on my own gnawed at me for some time. Helping Maria choose what to wear wasn't all bad. Painting Loago's nails every time wasn't bad either. At least I had a life. Now that I was alone, my day-to-day was pretty dull. No overspending. No partying. No alcohol. I lived like a minimalist for a while before I sought friends on social media. It seemed promising at first, but it didn't work out. I ended up being the sharer—sharing other people's posts and, just like Jacaranda, always too busy thinking about what to post next.

I went back to the three princesses, who were quick to reject me in unison as if they had been practicing the line, waiting for me to come crawling back.

"You don't just come and go as you wish!" they said to my face.

"It's okay, I can go back to my boring, crusty life," I replied.

I went to my room because Keolebogile had moved off campus and in with her boyfriend. I packed my books neatly in my backpack and went to the library. It was a holiday, and it was closed. Disappointed, I dragged my feet back to my room.

I slept for half an hour and woke up to booming music next door and muffled voices. I dragged my groggy self to the next room.

"I am trying to sleep. Can you turn it down a bit?" I asked.

"What the fuck? It's just a small celebration with my friends. I have a life to live, and you don't, so don't tell me how to live my life," she snapped.

I was just asking her to minimize the noise, and she overreacted, telling me I had no life. I dragged my feet back to my room, constantly checking my phone to see how my ex-friends were spending the night. Wherever they were, it was lit and they were having a blast, while I was stuck all alone with my problems chilling with me. My demons were glad I spent almost all my life with them. I had always thought that university would bring me bountiful friends since I was an outcast back in high school. Here I was, trying way too hard to belong to a group, to have people I could call friends. I wanted to be known too—not like a celebrity, but just to exist, to breathe the same air as everyone else. I tried too hard to fit in. Looking back at the times I did things to please my friends, to be known by others, I realized I overdid it. I lost myself and still got nothing. It was so pathetic to watch.

There was this guy. He smiled way too much and always noticed me. He always made my days. He would just come to say hi, smile, and say something sweet before he left. Not a week later, he was asking for favors. Wuhan was quite a spender, squandering his student allowance overnight, and I was there buying him breakfast and printing his assignments with my money. He also gave me hugs sometimes, but at the end of the day, I realized there was a price to pay for that smile, that hi, and that hug. It was too painful to watch, but I entertained him anyway—he was the first, and i bet the last guy who made girls swoon, who ever spoke to me, let alone shared the same space.

Keolebogile moved back and told me she would never leave me again. She was going to stick with me until the end of time. She said that guy must have done some voodoo to make her choose him over me, her best friend. My three friends also started texting way too much and acting weird. Just as I was about to fall for their lies, the *princesses*—Keolebogile too—began fighting over the guy who had been doing me favors in exchange for the last bits of my allowance. The three princesses went their separate ways. I really wished for Wuhan to mess with them, to show them they were nothing, to make them miserable. Not for any harm, but for someone to treat them the way they had treated me.

They constantly fought while I got to unknow and unmeet everyone else. When I was done, I embraced the lonely life. It was much *cooler* (the solo ride) than using the last of my allowance to buy friendship.

19

THE WHISPERING BONES

"Sometimes, the most haunting tales are the ones that nearly never see the light of the day." Unknown.

One day when I was ten years old, I got raped mercilessly by three grown men, married even. They had stared at me like hungry lions and devoured my body like wolves—they had menacing stares that made me even afraid to crawl into my insides, if it were possible.

I had looked up to them—they were well off and didn't even have to commute every morning. They had businesses they managed while sitting on the couch and watching Tom and Jerry re-runs. If you had seen them, you could have concluded they were young boys trapped in grown-ups' bodies.

I wanted to be like them when I grew up, rolling on the couch all day while money rolled into my accounts nonstop, so I spent a lot of time with them. It was all so I could save my poor family—

my mother had ten of us and she was single and a drunkard. She practically lived at the shebeen and I had to take care of all my siblings, some of whom were even older than me.

Just like usual, I woke up really early and went straight to my uncle's to clean his house, wash his laundry and plates, and he'd give me leftover foods and the expired tin stuff and meat he wasn't going to eat so I can fend for my family. I cleaned the house spotless, did the laundry and plates that were piled in the sink, and unusually, he asked me to stay longer. I obliged, assuming maybe his wife was coming from town so she would bring some stuff over and I would have a lot of food to carry home with me.

I stayed on the other couch and watched the television too, with them (uncle and his two friends). Once the show was over, they all cornered me on the couch and yanked my clothes and threw them away, and what followed is better left unsaid. I woke up hours later, with a pool of blood on the couch and a thundering headache. I couldn't feel my legs and I couldn't move at all. Their laughter echoed behind me, and they acted as if nothing had happened. I was silenced by a cup of rice and a wad of cash. I stayed quiet.

After graduating college, I ended up doing my internship back home. I ended up in a hospital, not far from home, and my supervisor was my uncle's firstborn. She'd loved me since I was a kid. I was smart and confident. We ended up stuck together, traveling together on her car and working together in the hospital. We would pass by Uncle's first before she dropped me at my place. The three musketeers were still rolling on couches and had upgraded from being babies to teenagers. They played video games all day and jerked off to the big-breasted women models in magazines.

"You've grown up to become a beautiful young woman," he muttered seductively, his hand making its way to my thighs. It slithered over my thighs and went all the way up to my bra. I shivered a little as nervousness snaked down my spine. Myriad fleeting emotions flickered in and out of me. His stare bore into my soul. The other one gave me an evil smirk.

My uncle was having a hearty conversation with his firstborn, who wanted to know why he was always with the two guys with a very bad reputation for sleeping around with children that were like their daughters in the village. They whispered and hushed each other multiple times before they came down, sweat trickling down their foreheads. I expelled a big sigh of relief, If I had stayed with these two impudent brats of men, maybe she would've found only my bones left there. Uncle gave me a threatening look.

"Girl, let's go," she announced.

I heaved up and headed to the car. She was hot on my tail, jingling the car keys. She drove me home and went back to their place. The next day, she wasn't going to drop me off and she asked me to pass by my uncle's to grab some of her things she'd left behind.

I went there and the same thing from twelve years ago happened. It happened multiple times and I had no one to tell. I'd just assumed it was bad timing because the other times I got there, they wouldn't bat an eye in my direction, and sometimes they'd jump me and devour me hungrily.

I squirmed against their grip, breathing heavily from the rough thrusting and sloppy *kissing*. They nearly chewed my lips and tongue away. The other one grabbed a handful of my hair and pulled my head back, as the other two pinned me down and alternated getting on top of me. A muffled "ouch" escaped through my teeth and I had broken the rule—not a sound I should produce. They whooped my bare ass and grabbed my breasts violently. Realizing how pathetic this situation was, I wished I would die or just perish. I strongly wished to just die at that moment because there was absolutely nothing left of me.

"Surpriseee," multiple voices bellowed at the same time. My uncle's wife and his children had visited unannounced—and talk about timing, I was pinned on the plush cushion, passed out, and the three musketeers surrounded me, their members pointed at me.

I heard Uncle's wife collapsed at the sight. I woke up three days later, the hospital ammonia smell piercing through my nostrils as I vomited all over the hospital bed. Police officers stood right next to my bed with test tubes and a duck-bill-shaped device. A streak of light shined through the entire room, like justice had just filtered through the blinds. They had a clipboard and a pen.

"Twelve years ago, I went to clean at my uncle's . . ."

I started and that was the end of the three musketeers.

20

CHINA DESTINY

"If you are falling apart, and I am falling apart, what is stopping us from falling apart together?" Neil, 27.

I had loved the new girl. She was nice and all that. She was unique. She was quiet and smiled a lot. I'd thought, what a great human being I'd bagged for life. What a marvelous person I'd met, and I'd never missed offering a few apples and some rice to the deity on the day we met. I burnt scented candles as well.

I had loved her whole. Fell in love at the speed of light and knocked out a few teeth from falling. How it started was uncanny. She had just moved into our compound because of her job, and we only exchanged greetings a couple of times. I had winked multiple times and hit on her, but she totally ignored me like I was some frog. She made me doubt myself for a while, then bamn, I fell into a trap. She was all sweet all of a sudden and acted like we were long-time besties. I'd loved the feeling that came with the sudden nice treatment.

She was my absolute crush, so I ended things with the girl I had been dating. I told her it was over and blocked her and erased everything related to her on my phone. I was just . . . just getting ready for the new relationship with the new girl.

She had told me her name was Melissa, and I'd wanted to marry her right away. "What a glamorous name and face you have there." I'd fallen head over heels! Next I told my guys to go have their suits tailored and be ready for a wedding, it was so inevitable. I'd told them how bright my future was with the bright woman I'd just discovered, like gold. Rare and beautiful.

We had moved really quickly. Moved into each other's house and slept together. We had talked about kids afterward. She told me she wanted her firstborn to be a boy, so she named him after Mbappe, the football star. I had told her I wanted a girl, and if I was to name her after anyone, it would have been my grandmother. She raised me my whole life until her last breath. She had snuggled closer to me and peppered my face with kisses.

Melissa said I was the sweetest guy she had ever met, and butterflies had swum in my stomach with trumpets.

We had dated like in the movies. Kissing in the rain. Watching the moon while holding hands. Sleeping on each other while using public transport. Going to restaurants and weird sex places. Taking long walks and hugging a lot in the darkness. We loved each other like the lead actor and lead actress in a Rom-com.

But she wasn't like lead actresses. She seldom said, "I love you" or "I miss you." She would say that only if I did. She never texted a good morning or anything of that sort. She just texted randomly any time she wanted. She would not call or text for two days straight and would come back and pick up our conversation from where it had ended like it was nothing. I didn't complain because I loved her. I trusted her.

She was barely interested in me. She never asked what I did for a living or what my name was and my age. But I'd hoped we would get to know each other as time went on.

Suddenly she asked for her house key she had given me. Later that day, she was all cuddly and smooching me nonstop as if nothing happened. She would go from fire to ice cold from time to time. I'd thought she must be a moody person. Little did I know about a bunch of stuff. That her real name wasn't Melissa. She didn't move here because of the job. She had moved because of a dog. The very same dog that held my destiny. Had I known, I could have been born as that dog.

Eventually, she was obsessed with wanting to visit her home village but couldn't because of her work schedule. If she wasn't talking about her home village, she talked about China. At first, genuinely, I had thought of the Asian country. It was talked about so highly. Then I'd thought it was a friend of hers. She had later corrected me and told me it wasn't China as in the country. It was China, but her entire universe. And it was a chihuahua in soulmate form. I'd snorted before she threw me a dangerous look. I held my breath for a second.

"Then what am I to you if a mere dog means the entire universe?"

She had just rolled her eyes in my direction and told me to chill. Later the same day, when the sun dipped, she appeared wearing a million-dollar smile with the chihuahua. The dog was wearing Gucci pants and a Gucci-branded name tag. Immediately upon seeing me, it started drama, barking and snarling like I'd stolen a piece of meat from her plate. She had told me to go to my house.

"Why are you chasing me away?"

"I am not chasing you away! I am just telling you to give me some space to be with China, and again, she doesn't seem to be very fond of you. Maybe give her some time . . ."

I raised my hands in exasperation and left quietly. That night, I tried apologizing to the girl I left. I tried finding a way to retrieve her number and contact her. She was still mad and didn't want anything to do with me. Melissa sent me a twenty-five-minute voice note, telling me over and over again how she thought we were not going to work because China didn't love me. She literally told me the chihuahua had been barking at the sweater I'd left behind all night until she lost her voice.

"If you don't wanna date me, just say it! Say it to my face!" I'd sent her a voice note, yelling like a crazed man.

She'd replied with with an "I am sorry, man, China doesn't wanna see you ever again, so yeah . . ."

"What the actual fuck are you saying?!"

My heart bled. I never knew I'd love someone that much. I tried crawling back to the girl I'd dumped, but she had found a "better" guy as she had said. I ended up stalking Melissa on Facebook, Instagram, everywhere, and that is how I learnt it wasn't about the chihuahua at all. I regretted hating it so much and even having a slight thought of killing the innocent pet. The girl was still hung up on her previous ex-boyfriend, and from her Instagram stories, I could tell she was barely coping. I regretted losing the girl I had before Melissa entered my life. She was kind and cool, just like Melissa.

"If you are falling apart, and I am falling apart, what is stopping us from falling apart together?"

At the end of the day, she never replied to my text. It was okay since I already knew the answer. She didn't want anything to do with me, and her silence absolutely meant, "We can fall apart separately."

21

MY HERO

"R.I.P. to my idiotic self." Tlamelo, 10.

From the day I was born, I'd never had a father figure in my life. The very moment my mother had whispered, "Rraago o gatilwe ke terena" in my ear, I knew I was different from all the other kids.

They had shoulders to cry on, protectors who shielded them from life's harshness, and providers who ensured they never went to bed hungry. They had someone to hold them close in the dead of night, whispering reassurances and chasing away their fears. But for me, it was always just my mother—my sole parent, my everything.

One evening, out of the blue, I turned to her and asked, "Mom, do you think our lives would be better if we had someone to protect and provide for us?" We were seated across from each other, the flames casting shadows on our faces. She gazed at the stars, silent yet attentive.

"What do you think, Tlamelo?" she finally replied, her eyes unyielding.

"Mama," I said, "if Papa were here, he'd fill our home with food, protect you from loan sharks'. He'd work tirelessly, provide for us, and ensure we never had to borrow from those sharks again." She'd looked at the empty space and never opened her mouth again for the rest of the night.

After enduring bullies at school, I'd sprint home, my heart racing with relief. Home was my sanctuary—a place where no one would mock me for falling from the sky. Despite the occasional visits from relentless loan sharks, our humble place still felt like home. They'd ransack our house, but we'd rearrange the pieces afterward. After all, we had very little to begin with.

One day, I mustered the courage to speak to my mother. Her bruised, swollen eye bore silent witness to her struggles. Her expression remained stoic, lips parting as if she might say something, yet nothing escaped them. I spoke matter-of-factly, suggesting two options: either we relocate and find a hidden refuge, or she finds someone—a protector—for us and our fragile home.

She continued her quiet labor, picking up the shards of our existence and restoring order.

The following day, slipping away from my cold-hearted colleagues, I raced home as always. But this time, the yard stood undisturbed, and my mother was nowhere to be seen. Panic surged within me, and I called out, my voice echoing through the empty rooms:

"Mama . . . Mama . . . where are you?"

My eyes widened as they fell upon a man perched on our makeshift chair made from a paint bucket. I scanned the room, seeking my mother, and there she was—seated on her favorite mat. Her voice trembled as she spoke my name.

"Tlamelo . . ." She hesitated, her gaze shifting toward the man.

"He saved me from the loan sharks," she whispered, her words barely audible.

I extended my hand to the stranger, my smile genuine. "Good afternoon, sir. Thank you for protecting my mother while I was away. May you stay by her side and be with her for a long time."

Deep inside, I thought, he was my hero.

He entered our lives when hope seemed scarce. Gradually, he earned our trust, becoming a permanent fixture in our humble home. He paid off my mother's debts, freeing us from the clutches of loan sharks and their beatings. A true hero, he saved us. Now, I walked through school with my head held high—I had a father. No longer did I feel like a child who fell from the sky; I was created just like everyone else, with both a man and a woman.

He taught me practical skills: fixing fences, hunting, and hard work. His warm hands enveloped mine, reassuring me that everything would be okay. In the dead of night, he chased away my terrors. Warm blankets and nourishing meals became my solace. Even in my darkest hours, I felt loved—a strength that anchored me. In exchange, I taught him to read and write, since he never went to school. I also taught him the dangers of smoking cigarettes, which he seemed to be so fond of, and he would listen attentively and call me his son. He promised me he was going to quit smoking soon as well.

But what happened to my hero, who burst into my life like a sudden storm? Someone, fetch the medics quickly!

One weekend morning, he roused me from slumber, declaring that weekends were for hunting hares and birds. I leaped up, slipped on my sandals, and led the way. But then, he vanished. Vanished like mist in the forest. I scoured every inch, my heart racing. One moment he was there, the next gone. Lost, I wandered too far, disoriented and exhausted. I collapsed, the spinning earth my only companion. Thirst clawed at my throat, and darkness closed in as I drifted into an uneasy sleep.

And then, a deer, a silent sentinel, roused me. Instinct kicked in; I stalked it, arrow ready. But when I released that arrow, it betrayed me, falling at my feet. Pain seared through my body— the arrow had found its mark. Blood oozed, and I staggered, legs weakening. I groaned, clutching the wound.

In my haze, I wondered, could another hunter have made this mistake? Would they come to my aid? Footsteps approached—a lifeline. My heart soared. Someone was coming to rescue me.

"Papa," I whispered, my eyes shining like a Christmas bulb as my hero stepped in to rescue me. He'd asked me to call him "father" for as long as he remained in my life. A tear slipped down my cheek, and a fragile smile tugged at my lips. But his response surprised me—he didn't return my smile. Instead, he regarded me as if I were a stranger. Retrieving his Nokia phone from his pocket, he pressed the buttons and retreated to a distance.

"Perhaps he's calling an ambulance," I thought, clinging to a glimmer of hope. I closed my eyes, seeking solace in the darkness, willing the pain away. The approaching sound of a car promised relief—I'd go to the clinic, eyes shut, and trust that my hero's presence would keep me safe.

"As long as he's there," I whispered inwardly, "I'll be okay."

Strong arms lifted me, depositing me into the car. I lay there, eyes closed, as the vehicle carried me. Abruptly, it halted. My body, drained of blood, felt lifeless; my vision blurred. Those same arms lifted me again, but this time, they threw me onto the ground.

"Why are the paramedics a little rougher today?" I wondered, gritting my teeth against the pain. I waited for an injection, a bandage—standard care. Instead, I found myself rolling on dry grass, discomfort gnawing at me. I tried to open my eyes, but only blurry shapes surrounded me.

"How much for this package?" a familiar voice echoed.

"Just a packet of cigar," came the reply.

"Sweet deal," he concluded.

He counted on his fingers, wearing the grin of a lottery winner. "These beautiful eyes—worth \$130,000. Two kidneys—\$150,000 each. A heart—\$5,000,000 . . ." My heart sank. "Sold? By whom?"

"Your hero," the voice answered.

Tears streamed sideways. Something sharp pierced my ribs, agony engulfing me. As they prepared to extract my valuable parts, a hand penetrated my rib-cage, gripping my heart, wrenching it from its roots. In that moment, I whispered a desperate prayer:

"God, my true hero, take me far away. Save me from these predators, this pain, this tragedy. I feel defeated, no longer needed."

As I slowly departed from this realm, I realized who my true hero was. The figure that appeared to embrace me as I floated in the clouds. It whispered, "I am your father, your uncle, your mother, your cousin—your everything."

22

WAITING

"Did you exist at all?" Merylin, 35.

Dear Ben,

While I waited for you, I might have counted all the stars, their distant glimmers like breadcrumbs leading me back to you. Scorpii, Orionis, Lyrae, Sirius—they became my companions in the quiet nights. I wove their names into constellations, hoping they'd spell out your arrival, and like an unexpected comet streaking across the sky, you would appear out of nowhere and say, "I told you not to wait for me. I told you that I will come. I will show up no matter how long it takes." In that moment, my heart would unfurl like a sail catching the cosmic winds. For there is no truth greater than this: You, with your promise, are my North Star—the unwavering guide through the vastness of waiting.

Why does it feel like I've been waiting for ages? I lingered in the house, unable to keep still. The parted curtains framed me like a ghost at the window, eyes fixed on the gate. I hoped it would creak open, but silence clung to the air no matter how long I waited. Eventually, weariness settled in, and I retreated to the porch. There, I replayed our last encounter—the words exchanged, the unspoken pauses. It felt like centuries ago, eons even. Yet, your laughter lingered, a delicate melody etched into the quiet spaces between my heartbeats. A cherished talisman, guarding me against encroaching shadows.

On that day, do you remember? You held my hands, whispered, "I'd be lost without you." And now, here I am—perched by the window, watching seasons change, wondering if you wandered off without me and got lost like the society our former president lamented (a society without its culture, a lost generation, he'd said). Curiosity tugs at me: Why this penchant for keeping me waiting? Waiting— an absolute ache, the slow unraveling of hope. Do you know its weight? Its hollow echo? Perhaps not. But I do. Oh, how I do.

A tightly wound knot tightens in my stomach with each passing moment. I check my phone repeatedly, steal glances at the clock—tick, tock, tick, tock. I rehearse my reaction for when I see you. Minutes stretch into hours, and hours feel like eternity as I toggle between optimism and pessimism, clinging to hope while bracing for disappointment. I pray that you'll come to see me now. I attempt distractions—books, movies, folding laundry, pacing—but nothing truly works without you here. When night descends, I lie awake, staring at the ceiling. My mind flits from one memory to another, unsure which to settle upon. Sometimes my brain feels like it's about to explode, and my heart pounds at the mere thought of you.

Do you like it when I suffer? When I am losing my mind? When I look like a raccoon from lack of sleep?

Will you show up this time? With that same smile, the one you left imprinted on my heart? The aura you carried, like stardust woven into your very being. Whisper to me when you're coming, and I'll slip into my best dress. I'll wait for you at the crossroads of time, where moments intersect and memories collide. And when you arrive, I'll hug you tightly, I'll tell you how much I've missed you, and then, with lips trembling, I'll kiss you, and tell you what you mean to me—galaxies, everything there is in this world.

P.S. I will be waiting for you.

-The reply from Ben, six years later-

Dear Merylin,

Before you turn into a skeleton waiting, find someone else. I had clearly mentioned: DO. NOT. WAIT. FOR. ME, idiot.

23

ANNE

"Mama this, mama that,' we murmur, our voices a fragile chorus as we gather around your resting place." Penelope, 32.

I wonder how you felt all those years, hearing us call you by your name while we referred to grandmother as "mother." It doesn't seem fair now, especially, that I have a daughter who calls me by my first name and has no one to call "mother" since you are gone. As I navigated motherhood, the depth of your patience and love hits me harder. It pains me that I never acknowledged it fully while you were here. You showed me what true strength looks like. It wasn't just enduring the physical pain but also in the way you handled the emotional wounds we unknowingly inflicted on you.

The anguish of hearing the child you bore never call you mama must have been more than that of the cancer that saved you from us. It is incredible how you never complained or corrected me, big brother, and the siblings that came after us. You always answered when we called you by your name and smiled when we called grandmother "mama." I remember when your friend visited and, hearing us call you "Anne," said, "Disown these kids." You just laughed it off, saying that at the end of the day, we knew who our mother was.

You said, "I have taught them every woman they will ever cross paths with will be mother as well, and I wouldn't disown my kids just because they called you mother." She didn't seem like she would tolerate that in her life. At least just before you left, my nephew called you mama. That must have made your heart skip a beat for the first time in your life, and now I see why you wanted him named Blessing. He was indeed god-sent, bringing you joy and breathing life into your days, so that more blessings could come and call you mama.

We never once said thank you for bringing us into this life. We never took you out on a nice date, never celebrated your birthdays. Now it is too late. We cannot celebrate you; we weep on your death anniversary. Partly because we never appreciated you when you were alive. We never showed you we were proud of who you were to us. Some kids never had mothers, or rather loving and caring mothers like you, yet we had you who gave us your all, and yet we never said, "Thank you, Mother" or did anything for you.

And now, we live in regret. We could have done this, we could have done that while you were still alive. I remember that time when you were picking up litter at my school, and I was so embarrassed of you. I told my classmates I didn't know who you were. It plays over and over in my head, every second, and I should say, "I am sorry, Mom, you were that kind of a person—the kind who would do anything for people who never did anything for her, even when were grown." On your deathbed, you fought with every fiber of your being to stay for us, the very same unappreciative brats you called your babies.

Every day, I kneel and pray to the almighty God, asking for another chance so we can call you Mom, say, "Thank you, Mother," and treat you like a queen, just once. You didn't deserve the way we treated you—like you were a nobody. We always say, given another chance, we would do anything to learn to treat you better, to treat you right.

Before I slip into slumber, the echoes of your laughter gently lull me into a deep sleep. I hear your voice say something sweet, followed by that laughter of generations. So, dear Anne, dear Mama, your legacy lives on, in the love and strength you instilled in us. I see it now, and I hope wherever you are, you know how deeply you are cherished and remembered.

May you rest, knowing that our love transcends mountains and that your heart still beats within ours.

24

THE FASTEST RUNNERS ALIVE?

"The devil long lost his powers." Uebert Angel.

I have seen Letsile Tebogo run. I have seen the guy from America run—I forgot his name, the tall, dark one with beads on his hair. Lyles? I have heard Bolt is the fastest one though, but what I see here is beyond the fastest. If these guys were invited to the Olympics, they would just be given the whole Earth afterward, and they would even own us. But again, I think they already own the world, looking at the speed they possess; they own the world and us all together.

Who are these guys? That was the question that was supposed to have come to my mind first instead of being amazed by their speed. I was headed to hell here, and honestly, I wasn't supposed to be standing there, screaming and cheering at the top of my lungs. When will I ever be serious in my life? I wondered. Wait a minute, the right question is: How am I still the same even in the afterlife? Can you imagine I was about to be thrown in the fire, yet I was there whooping like a donkey?

I didn't have a problem with dying unfairly, dramatically, and stuff, but I had a problem with how things turned out. I had been in a queue for as long as I had been dead. A very long queue. I had been there for years listening to people tell each other stories about how they died, how they miss their relatives, the riches they left behind, how they wish they could have led better lives—blah, blah, blah—and all they were sure of was that the queue on that long, long road was headed to Heaven.

"Look at these babies."

"Look at that pastor from the TV. He was a great pastor, millions and millions of followers . . ."

"Look at this . . . See that . . ."

"That is enough proof that we are headed to Heaven," they had said.

I listened to them tell stories about their lives with smiles and never told them my story. It was pathetic to tell. All these people who told stories had achieved big in their lives and lived like legends. How they had fought wild boars and leopards and defeated them. How they had run well from the north, east, west, and south. How they had conquered. It was all stories of victory, like they were never, even once, on a losing team. Some stories were exaggerated, though I would snort from time to time and try with all my might not to laugh like a hyena.

At the end of it all, I'd realized only one thing: these people, or should I say ghosts, told stories that had kept us going for years and years without us knowing. It was like summer had passed a million times. Winter, too. Spring and autumn, but you know, since now we were in the underworld, I don't know if they still went with the same names or something more sinister since we were in hell.

When the huge gates finally appeared, we had cheered knowing we were closer, getting closer to joining the others who were already enjoying the fruits and chilling with elephants in the much-anticipated paradise in Heaven. Once we were in, we couldn't hide our excitement. We chatted loudly about what we will do when we are mixed with animals and every other race there.

"I am going to befriend a Taiwanese."

"I am going to eat all the fruits in the Garden of Eden all night long until God himself decides to send me back to Earth."

"It would be fun if we were all naked, so we could see whose size is . . ." I stifled a laugh.

Excitement can make you speak languages you've never even heard before. It will cause people to blabber nonsense like they're delusional—like you're supremely high on very illicit drugs. We snapped back to reality when we heard someone screaming like a mad person, and human-like figures with wings appeared out of nowhere to chase a ghost running for its already perished life.

"We're all headed to Hell!"

"We're all going to die!"

Wait a minute, aren't we all dead already?

Chaos ensued as everyone tried to escape. The winged figures chased them as if they'd been doing this forever and were very aware of people like Isaac Makwala and Nigel Amos, ready to engulf them and fly away. I stood there, amazed. Damn, that was fast! I thought I could have been an athlete, running my whole life just to show off here—maybe I could have become a legend. I could have run and run, proving I wasn't just breathing and doing nothing on Earth. My dreams looked at me with sorrowful eyes. Run from who? Us? But isn't that what you've specialized in your whole life—running away, hiding from us?

"Stop lying; you'll end up in Hell like me! I ran from my never-ending problems, not from my dreams!"

"You said you would turn us into reality before you died—in past lifetimes and the last one too. But you kicked us aside, told us we weren't worth your time or attention . . ."

"See, I was too tired, guys. How many lifetimes did you mention? If it were you, wouldn't you be tired?"

I rolled my eyes in disgust. "Wait, I want to witness all this, so when I get another chance, I can tell those on Earth how fast these guys can run."

I turned to watch the *chaos* as these ghosts were taken back to where they belonged. Strangely, there was nobody with horns or pitchforks—just a gigantic fire. People were thrown into the flames like firewood, while the master of all that is sinister roared, howling and screaming, his body bound by chains like some sort of Marvel superhero suit, preventing him from escaping at all as he burnt and burnt . . . for eons, he burnt.

25

DEAR FELLOW MEN

"God forgive me, but I truly hope *that woman* meets a fate as grim as Jezebel's, with her body devoured by dogs in the end."
Trevor, 59.

Before I knew it, I had taken everything my father left me and donated it all as dowry. I was going to marry the woman of my dreams, the most beautiful woman with features of a Greek goddess. She moved with grace that made her hips sway as if they were playing to a secret melody. She was a deaconess in my church, and partly the reason I never missed church. Her smile was warm and welcoming, and she held everyone's hands with genuine affection. I was terrified that all the other brothers had their eyes on her, and if I didn't act quickly, someone else would marry her. They might even keep her from coming to church, believing she was too precious to be seen or touched by anyone else. If it were allowed, they might have her dress like a Muslim woman, wear gloves too so she would not come into contact with us.

Who knew coming to church would be this helpful? Imagine if I had stayed glued to the Will and Sons director's chair without stepping out. I don't even want to think about it because I wouldn't have discovered the gem I found the moment I left that chair.

I had found a wife, and everyone was overjoyed when I announced our plans. The congregation clapped and kissed our hands to bless us. We were getting married.

"You haven't known her for a week, and now you're announcing that you're marrying her? Are you sure about this, Trevor?" Maps, my secretary, asked after I told him about my plans to marry Martha.

"Come on, man, I've found my missing rib," I said, a small smile creeping onto my lips. "And you should jump up and say congratulations, Mr. Director. You finally won't be jerking off to the wall anymore," I continued.

Maps just huffed and congratulated me, his face clearly showing he was half against the idea, or maybe totally.

The company was thriving, with investors flocking to us, bringing in substantial funds. My life seemed almost too perfect. The only downside was my solitude; I was growing old alone. At my age, I needed a wife more than money. Church seemed the ideal place to find a good woman. That's where I found Martha. I loved her and wanted to marry her immediately. After the pastor approved our relationship, we announced our plans and proceeded with the formalities. I married her, using all the cattle my dad had left me as dowry. I transferred some of my buildings and shares to her name, and we now held equal shares in Will and Sons Holdings Group. I was head over heels and devoted to caring for her for the rest of my life.

The first five years were perfect. We had a baby despite her initial reluctance, as she didn't want to become a granny. It took nearly a year of convincing, but she finally agreed, and a year later, she gave birth to the bountiful heir of Will and Sons Holdings Group. I couldn't contain my happiness and invited my colleagues for a small celebratory party at our house. Celebrations followed each year as we welcomed more children—two more boys and a baby girl. She seemed relieved after giving birth to a princess after two tries.

I now had to work harder since I had six people to care for, including myself. With inflation rising, our daily expenses were becoming increasingly burdensome. My kids attended the most expensive schools, each costing nearly a million per term. My wife needed a lot of money for jewelry and expensive clothes to match the wives of other directors and business tycoons. This demanded that I work extra hard, often without sleep, which wasn't possible at all. I had spent all my fortune, and my accounts were nearly at zero. Maybe I should have stayed alone forever?

"Honey, I was thinking, maybe our children could go to Soar Academy. It's not as expensive as Lions Academy."

She snapped, "In your dreams."

I froze, retracing my words to see if I had said something senseless.

"At this rate, we might go bankrupt. Can you please stop buying everything you see online? Half the time, the actual thing doesn't look like the picture, and you've wasted a wad of cash—"

"What happened to working hard? Didn't you say you would work hard for both of us?"

"I do work really hard, okay?"

"Then why are you whining and nagging at me? Are you tired of taking care of me and my kids already?"

"Look, Martha, I will never get tired of taking care of you and our babies, okay?"

"Then stop whining."

I just ignored her. She could be a little edgy sometimes, especially when she was on her menses. I started pouring all my energy into the company, chasing after investors and working extra hours. The only time I saw my family was when we went to church. After church, I would head back to the company headquarters and work my ass off. Whenever I found some time, I would rush home to dine with my family. Surprisingly, Martha had been edgy and easily irritated by everything I said and my presence.

"Exactly how long did her period last this time?" I wondered as

I stole glances in her direction. She gave me the cold shoulder as she cleaned the kitchen.

"Are you mad at me?"

She snapped, "No!" in my direction and demanded I transfer my shares to her. I didn't negotiate or try to get on her nerves. The next day, after holding a board meeting and transferring my shares, I jumped into my orange Rubicon, turned the key in the ignition, and went to see her uncle. When I got there, it was bad news. The neighbor told me the man who lived next door, supposedly Martha's uncle, had died a year ago. Why hadn't she mentioned anything about it? I brushed it off my mind.

"He looked so vibrant. How did he die?" I asked.

"Car accident," the neighbor replied.

I went back to the company and worked extra hours before officially knocking off. I passed by the shopping mall to get some veggies before heading home.

"I'm home," I announced upon arrival, but no one answered. Not even Lucy came running to the door to ask what I brought from work for her.

"Lucy?" I called out, my voice bouncing off the walls. I strutted into the kitchen and dropped the vegetables on the counter. I headed straight to the bedroom, took off my clothes, and went right into the shower. Ten minutes after stepping into the shower, I heard the living room door creak and the sounds of the kids rushing into the house, followed by the sound of a car.

"Honey," I said as I stepped into the bedroom, finding Martha struggling to remove her earrings.

"Hi," she answered without looking in my direction.

"Hey, what's up? Are we good?"

"Why? Are we supposed to be good?"

I trudged over and stood behind her, squeezing her shoulders in an attempt to massage them. She yanked and swatted my hands away like they had thorns.

"I guess we are not good . . . Wanna talk about it?"

"Not at all."

"And whose car was leaving the compound a while ago?"

"That should be the least of your concerns . . . Don't even pretend to care or give me attention, because you love your company more—you lied to my face."

"What is this all about?"

She stood up, hauled her feet from the mat, and pulled the covers over her body.

"No dinner today?"

She stayed quiet. I trudged to the kitchen to grab a cup of coffee.

The next day, I came home to silence again. I was too tired and went straight to bed. The next morning, I went to work and came back to nothingness in the house. Not a sound, nothing. I waited the whole night, but neither Lucy nor Martha came home.

The next day, I went to the company, but it was no longer mine. There was an emergency board meeting. Martha had become the new owner overnight, and the shares said it all. Before I knew it, my house was no longer mine, my children were not mine, and everything I had worked hard for all these years came crumbling at my feet. I decided to see Pastor Genesis for advice and a one-on-one deliverance session.

When I got there, the place had changed into a butchery.

"Where did the church move to?" I asked the big man guarding the place.

"I heard they disbanded."

"Disbanded? C'mon, dude, say something worth hearing. This was not some pop band."

"I heard the pastor quit. Found a new calling."

"You know what, forget about it."

I left, tried calling the pastor to no avail. Tried the deacons, no luck. Even some members of the church whose numbers I had . . . nothing. That's when realization hit me like a train. From the young uncle with a brown jacket to Pastor Genesis, to everyone involved—it was a perfectly planned scam. It all began with Pastor Genesis inviting me to church, then bam, the most beautiful woman in the church is not married, the pastor too, that stupid comedian guy from Facebook who played the uncle. How did I miss the same brown jacket from all his photos?

"Shit . . . shit," I spat a string of profanities, heading back to the company headquarters.

"You are not allowed here, and if you resort to physical force, there are police officers already in the building to take care of that immediately, as the new madam said it might tamper with the sales of the company. Thank you."

"What?"

I looked at the new security officer.

I lost it. I harrassed them all. Burnt the place down.

Immediately after being released from the psychiatric hospital, I went straight to Facebook to tell the world my story and warn men.

"Dear fellow men . . ."

I started typing, but I couldn't write anything anymore as the phone kept acting up from all the tears I had shed. Every word rolled with a tear hitting the screen. I had lost everything, and there was nothing left of me. I stopped at some stall, pretended to ask for directions, and managed to steal rat poison while the woman was busy with some geography.

"Thank you. I think I know the way to where I want to go."

With that, I took a left turn instead of the right turn she had said I should take. I tore the corner of the powder packet and swallowed the rest without a sliver of hesitation. I felt something rearrange my insides, chopping them . . .

26

HEADHUNTER QUOTE 2

"While I have no one to call a friend, can I by chance, at least, have somebody, something, I will search for, from a group, at the end of the day?" Headhunter101.

27

THE MO TAE GOO EFFECT

"There is nothing more dangerous than someone with nothing left to lose." Mo Tae Goo, Voice, 1.

"Who are..." The investigator barely began his question before the menacing gentleman curtly cut him off.

The gentleman said, "calling me a copycat is disrespectful. Serial killer? That's closer to the truth, but my fans call me Master. I tolerate them for now because they are like family. There will come a time when I will knock some sense into those chicken heads. Slaughter them all! Because I am the only truth, the chosen one.

"I am the light, the way, the Punisher, and honestly, when I say such things, adrenaline shoots to my brain and makes me dizzy. Makes me feel like I am flying. Maybe, just maybe, I possess some sort of superpowers. They make me want to kill you all and rise, become the devil's right-hand man."

"Why did you kill the prosecutor?" the investigator asked.

"Initially, I only wanted to chop off the hand that wrote the arrest warrant, but I got carried away because he had such a pretty face, you know. I sliced him into fine pieces, just like the fine man he was. It was really, really fun. You won't believe this, but he fought for his life until the very end. Even the pieces of his body nearly found a way back to each other and came back to life miraculously, beating the odds!"

He continued, "You would have felt underestimated too. Who dares set a trap for the Chosen One? Who dares play games with the Slaughterer of all things! Detective, if you had done that, I swear to my god, Mo Tae Goo, it could have put your whole family in jeopardy. I could have put you all in a cauldron and boiled you to death."

The investigator grabbed a recorder from across the table and pressed the red button.

"I heard your colleagues call me the madman. A psychopath. Show some love, people! Where are they? I would love to meet them. Show them some madman art. Show them what I am capable of and see if you can catch me. Funny, huh? How you guys cannot incarcerate me. The statute of limitations has long expired, and you funny detectives haven't even found the thirty-seven bodies I buried on your premises."

"What happened to you? Psychiatry evaluation shows you are not a psychopath."

"What happened to me?" I stayed quiet for a moment, maintaining the wicked smirk plastered across my face. A facade. Deep down inside, I wanted to scream, bawl my eyes out, but I instantly remembered I am a monster. I have always been a monster in everybody's eyes. They always said I had the looks of a serial killer, a rapist, and that I looked really ugly, like someone destined for destruction. People treated me like an alien, like I didn't have tear ducts or veins that run warm blood. Now my veins only run cold water, and my heart is as cold as ice with snow falling year after year. I am turning into the grim monster they always assumed I was. It's funny—now they all look scared for real.

I turned to the investigator. "I am just a man with nothing left to lose, and behaving like that man, I learned it from TV. Have you watched Voice, season one? There's a guy there, Mo Tae Goo, real name Kim Jae Wook. Very handsome. You've heard of inspirations and role models, right? He is more than that to me. He is my god. And who is your god, Detective? Gandhi?"

"I am an atheist," the detective answered.

"No wonder I liked you from the start. So, non-believer, I have some cleaning to do. Lean closer, I'll give you a hint. 10 p.m. sharp. The abandoned building near the filling station. Red jacket. Six hundred pounds. Rolex watch. Wait . . . I nearly gave you all the details. The rest is for you and your team to figure out. Unlike you all, I am the guy who is really good at what he does. See you when you have enough evidence to put me behind bars. *Annyeong, issaekdeul.*"

28

THE GHOSTS FROM NOWHERE

"The Devil and I got along just fine." Michael, 39.

Just when people started complaining about the sweltering heat more than unemployment, some ghosts landed in the town. Nobody knew where they came from. They were like missionaries, except they didn't preach. Instead, they built huge amusement parks and kindergartens where kids were exposed to virtually every language spoken on Earth. They taught children how to play instruments, act, and sing from a very young age. I heard they came because they wanted to elevate the country to a level where it could compete internationally and gain global recognition. Total twist of events—no one has ever seen these masterminds who were also teaching people how to dodge the sweltering heat. They had hired the people we knew to convince us they had good intentions.

Everyone was very excited and began criticizing the long-standing education system, calling it names like "murderer of destinies" and "poor system." They seemed to have forgotten that the same people who had come now were the ones who had come in the past, proclaiming that education was the future. Now, they had returned with the same promises, just dressed differently.

It wasn't even a week after their kindergartens started operating when kids began dying mysteriously. They were disappearing and killing each other mercilessly due to the fierce competitions they were forced into. After a musical night, one child who had lost the competition burned another little girl's dress while she was still wearing it. While everyone was waiting for the announcement of the winners, the actual winner had already died and been taken to the mortuary because her little body was in a very bad state. Weird incidents kept recurring, from kids poisoning each other to suddenly getting sick. After precisely a week, the medical reports would indicate multiple organ failure, leading to the child dying in a pitiful state.

Kids were not the only ones affected. Almost all their teachers and caretakers were reported to be seeing a mysterious therapist who gave them sleeping pills and injections that turned them into zombies, puppets who hallucinated and killed kids. They lured and kidnapped children at the amusement park. That's how I ended up locked in the middle of nowhere with all these people who had been kidnapped. Mothers, kids, young boys, and girls—I bet I was the oldest one here. This place was filled with young blood, and at 39, I was the old blood that ended up in this hellish place. First, because I was the kind who would never be silenced about what I had seen—I was a journalist. Second, I was in the wrong place at the wrong time. A teenage mother got kidnapped with her baby, I witnessed it, and I got kidnapped too.

I had escaped from these zombies multiple times, but at the end of the day, I would end up in the hands of another zombie. The whole country was involved, from politicians to police officers, old geezers, and even innocent kids. I ended up locked in a prison-like place, being fed drugs and water, talking gibberish. At least I was still sane, while everyone else in here wandered aimlessly and blacked out from time to time. I saw a guy who had been on the television for a year now, and to this day, he was still missing.When I approached him, they told him not to listen to me because I was not in the right state of mind. I tried talking to someone else, but it was the same—everyone was told I was the most sick person in that room and they shouldn't pay me attention.

One day, while I was dizzy and wandering around, praying desperately, I stumbled upon a little boy being dragged out of a room with doors like an escalator. He was practically a corpse, being hauled by two women towards that dreaded door from which no one ever returned. In an instant, I recognized him. He was my son, Junior, and the woman wailing in that elevator-like room was my wife. I attempted to save my only son, but I ended up in an office, negotiating with a voice so familiar it was etched in the back of my mind, like someone I had just spoken to. They called my son a package and threatened to kill my wife if I tried to save him(my son). That's when I stole the paper and ink. They promised me my wife would be safe, but in the end, I realized I had made a fool of myself by believing them. Junior was gone. My wife too, and I knew I was next.

That's how I ended up swallowing this piece of paper. They said I was a useless piece of meat they were going to feed to the wild dogs. If you are reading this, I believe the wild dogs don't feed on paper. Warn the people not to send their kids to these new, popular kindergartens. Protect the younger generation! At this rate, they will perish, and that will be the end. There will be no tomorrow.

29

THE VOICES IN MY HEAD

"I must give you life, demons." Pam, 49.

It is a lot of voices in my head. Some say this is not where you belong, others say you are not cut out for this, others make loud mockery laughter—howling like hyenas. Others tell me to stop, that I am just wasting my time. That I am a failure, a loser, and I am nothing. None among these voices is a bit kind. But there is this little voice from deep within me that whispers, go . . . go softly but where?

I remember the last interview I went to, centuries ago. That woman had smiled and fueled my hopes with a, "We will get back to you soon." That line was only enough to turn me into the trash queen who rummaged through trash for bottles. I sold bottles until I could make enough to afford a decent suit for my first ever job since graduating college ages ago. I waited for them to get back to me soon, like that woman had promised. Nothing came and my stress doubled. Depression came along, without a therapist, clearly pretending not to be aware I could not afford one.

For a very long time, I'd succumbed to depression and still nothing came. Only the voices of despair; they became louder and louder with each passing day. Even when everybody had forgotten about me, they seemed not to forget about me—like I was the love of their life.

Was I? Like the reason they felt alive? Like I gave them life? They took it away...I will overcome th...

30

HEADHUNTER101 QUOTE 3

"Everyone is lonely. But instead of coming together and celebrating life together, by chasing away loneliness altogether, we just wanna hurt and break and tear each other."
Headhunter101.

31

DAILY REMINDER TO SELF

"Never look down to test the ground before taking your next step; only he who keeps his eyes on the far horizon will find the right road." Dag Hammarskjold.

32

ABOUT THE AUTHOR

Headhunter101 was born in September 1999 and holds a bachelor's degree in Generic Nursing. With one year of experience as a nurse, she has just embarked on her professional journey in healthcare. From a young age, Headhunter101 has been passionate about writing, often receiving praise for her storytelling skills.In addition to her nursing career, Headhunter101 is an entrepreneur and the CEO of the Headhunter101 clothing brand. When she's not working, she enjoys reading, writing, and volunteering. Headhunter101 currently resides in Masunga, Botswana, with her family and their beloved mixed-breed Tswana and Chihuahua dog.

33

To The One Who Watches Over Me...

Do not let me fall apart.